JOY ON THE MOUNTAIN PEAK

CALL OF THE ROCKIES ~ BOOK 10

MISTY M. BELLER

ISBN-13 Trade Paperback: 978-1-954810-60-0

ISBN-13 Large Print Paperback: 978-1-954810-61-7

ISBN-13 Casebound Hardback: 978-1-954810-62-4

Be merciful unto me, O God, be merciful unto me:
for my soul trusteth in thee:
yea, in the shadow of thy wings will I make my refuge,
until these calamities be overpast.

Psalm 57:1 (KJV)

CHAPTER 1

"*H*e needs one more rock on his head. A big one."

Ben Lane pressed against the boulder, hiding him from the women as he replayed their words in his mind. Something rang familiar in the hushed tone of one of them, like the aroma of a favorite dessert he hadn't eaten in years. As it happened, he hadn't eaten *any* of his favorite foods in years. Two full years, in fact, since he and his sister had left Illinois to go west and become missionaries to the Indian tribes.

That's about how long it had been since he'd heard that same half-whisper, half-frantic tone.

It couldn't be.

The sounds of stones clanking drew his focus back to what might be happening on the other side of his hiding spot. Surely they weren't striking a man on the head with a rock.

He shifted to peer around the boulder. Two figures were working over a cluster of rocks. Both wore long skirts, not the

1

knee-length buckskin that clad the women in the Gros Ventre village.

White women.

Ben's mind struggled to catch up with what his eyes took in. It wasn't as if he hadn't seen white women recently. His sister was with him, after all. And there was Lola, who, along with her Shoshone husband, had been working as a translator for them this past year. But both Elise and Lola had taken to wearing buckskins through the winter. Leather was much warmer through these long frigid months. Far more practical, as well, and the two didn't stand out as much from the people they lived and worked among.

Which made these two strangers he'd stumbled upon stand out all the more. They looked like they'd stepped from a shop on Main Street in Marcyville. What were they doing in this wilderness, at least two months' journey from any form of civilization?

One of the women turned away from the pile of rocks, staying partly bent as she scanned the ground.

A jolt of recognition swept through him. He'd been right. But how could...?

His mind stuttered to a slow crawl even as an ache pressed in his chest—pain he'd worked hard to push aside for two years. One glimpse of her brought it all back like an avalanche.

Her gaze raked the grass around her, then lifted to the hedge of stones and brush that blocked her position from view on three sides. Before he could duck away, her eyes caught on his.

He froze, a rabbit confronted by a fox. Yet she was no fox, as much as the sight of her made his throat clog and a spurt of panic sweep through him.

How in the world had Heidi found him out here in this mountain wilderness?

～

*H*eidi Wallace stared as her pulse thundered through her neck.

Those eyes. When she'd first caught sight of him, she thought they were being attacked by natives. But her heart needed only a single beat before she recognized that intense gaze. The brown eyes she'd seen in her dreams so many nights since he left.

As Benjamin Lane slowly stepped from behind the boulder, she straightened to her full height and squared her shoulders. Part of her had known there was a chance—albeit a slim one— she might run into him if she traveled west with Philip, no matter how vast this country stretched. It seemed a cruel joke that she and Ben would be tossed together once more.

But perhaps they really truly were intended for each other, no matter how much of a rapscallion he'd been back in Marcyville. A tiny sprig of hope tried to take root in her heart at that idea, but she pressed the emotion back down. She'd spent far too long working to get over this man to ever allow him space in that particular organ again.

Heartbreaking as it was to see him, it was good they'd met now. At last, she could finally get answers.

Ben stood there, not a dozen steps away, watching her. His eyes were impossible to read, and the beard that covered his face shielded his expression. The scruff made him look like one of the mountain men they'd met along the journey up the Missouri River, especially with the leather clothing he wore. But this was just a costume, a slight shift of appearance that covered the Benjamin she'd known for so long.

Loved for so long.

"Who is it, Heidi?" Temperance's low question, filled with fear, broke through her thoughts and drew Ben's attention to her friend.

Heidi shifted so she could see them both, then lifted a hand to motion toward each as she made formal introductions. "Miss Temperance McDonough, may I present Mr. Benjamin Lane." She raised her brows at Ben. "Or should I say Reverend Lane now?"

A flush pinkened his ears. At least he had the good sense to be embarrassed, though the color could be sunburn from living outside all the time.

He shook his head as his eyes turned earnest. "I'm no minister. Just a man working to tell a lot of nice people about the God who loves them."

Tenderness pecked at her resolve. That was the Benjamin she'd known, the boy who'd simply wanted to help others, whether it be a study session to aid the new girl in catching up at school or inviting that same lonely young woman home for Sunday lunch with his family to help her feel like she belonged.

Heidi couldn't allow him to barrel through her defenses so easily. She'd learned her lesson well. She'd not let him injure her again.

Standing a little straighter, she nodded, then finished the introductions. "Mr. Lane then. Miss McDonough is assisting me on the journey."

A glance at Temperance showed she watched Heidi with one auburn brow raised. She must have picked up on the fact that Heidi had introduced *Ben* to *her*, not the other way around. In polite society, that would mean Temperance held the higher position, which would be a set-down to Ben. Perhaps he'd not picked up on the detail, but her friend certainly had. Heidi let the corner of her mouth twitch so Temperance would know she'd done it on purpose.

When Heidi turned her attention back to Ben, he was eyeing the mound of rocks behind her. A fresh wave of emotion swept through her. Poor Philip. His life was cut so short, and he'd suffered so much in his last hours.

How should she explain the situation to Benjamin? Would he realize those stones covered a grave?

The lines at his eyes had tightened. The knot at his throat worked as he swallowed. Then he nodded toward the rocks. "Is there someone buried under there?"

He didn't shift his focus to her, just kept his gaze locked on the mound. At least that allowed her to breathe while she scrambled for an explanation.

But Temperance's voice broke the silence, her Irish brogue rolling out with its usual lilting cadence. "Why t'at's her husband, sir. Mr. Philip."

Heidi locked her jaw to keep from wilting with dismay. That was the line they'd all agreed to give, but not to *Benjamin Lane*.

His eyes widened as they shifted to her, and the incredulity there almost covered the hurt that glimmered beneath.

Oh, if only she could melt into the ground like snow in summer. She forced herself to hold his gaze. To keep her chin high.

She might have some explaining to do, but so did he.

CHAPTER 2

*H*eidi watched Ben's gaze shift as more emotions seemed to flash through him. Did he recall that her cousin's name was Philip? Did he wonder if she'd met and married another man with the same name? He was probably scanning a mental list of all the people they'd known back in Marcyville.

She might as well stop those spinning thoughts.

A sigh slipped out as she glanced back at Philip's grave before meeting Ben's gaze again. "He's my cousin. You know Philip."

Ben's eyes rounded, a bit of horror creeping over his features. "You married your cousin?"

She grimaced. "Of course not." She shot a look at Temperance. "We only agreed to say that when we came west."

His brows lowered as his gaze moved back to the mound of rocks. "So that really is Philip?" His tone dropped, sadness slipping in.

A knot rose back into her throat, and she let her focus linger on the grave. "Sadly, yes."

This wasn't supposed to happen. Philip had been so worried

for her safety, she'd had to work hard to talk him into letting her come along on this assignment. Neither of them thought *he* would be the one to succumb to this wild country. Especially when they'd barely begun their work mapping the Marias River.

"What happened?" Ben's voice held a raw edge.

Philip had been six years older than she and Ben, away at university for the first two years after Heidi came to stay with her aunt and uncle in Marcyville. After that, her cousin traveled almost continually as he assisted a cartographer before starting his own business.

Ben had never been close to her cousin, but perhaps the reminder of someone from home, or simply of how quickly this wilderness could take a life, had sobered him.

"Rattlesnakes bit him."

Ben's gaze jerked to her face. "More than one?"

She nodded as the awful memory slipped in. Her chest tightened but she forced out the explanation. "He must've walked into a nest of them sunning on the rocks. He started screaming and ran. We..." Her throat clenched with a spasm. "We counted four bites." The sight of his blackened, swollen body had been almost too much to bear. Even now, bile rose at the image burned into her mind.

"Oh, Heidi." Ben's quiet words made it clear he was also visualizing the horror.

She shook her head to clear the thought and took a step back. "It was an awful way to die. He didn't deserve it, but we're trying to at least give him a decent burial." An idea slipped in, and she eyed him. Though she no longer trusted Ben Lane, as the son of a minister and a missionary himself, he would be far more capable to speak a funeral service over Philip's grave. "Would you mind saying a few words and a prayer for him?"

Ben's throat worked, his lips pressed together, yet he nodded. "Of course. But..." He glanced behind him. "Elise is here

7

too, back in the village. She'll want to see you. To come pay her respects."

Heidi's insides tightened. Elise was Ben's older sister, closer to Philip's age than her own. She'd probably known him well since they both grew up in Marcyville. She'd always been kind to Heidi, but that was *before*. Had whatever caused Ben to turn against her also done the same with Elise?

"She'll be overjoyed to see you." Ben's quiet voice broke through as though he'd listened in on her thoughts. He'd always had that ability.

Heidi drew herself up. She'd have to do better at guarding her emotions. He wasn't the man she'd once thought him to be.

She gave a single decisive nod. "Of course. Bring her for the service." Then she turned away to hoist up the rock she'd dropped and laid it atop the others. "How long will it take you to fetch her?" She kept her back to him and her voice casual.

"An hour, or maybe two. The village isn't far." Ben's voice sounded odd. Strained maybe.

It no longer mattered to her whether he was uncomfortable or what he thought. "We'll wait here." She moved to a cluster of wildflowers growing a few steps away. As she stooped to pick a handful, she kept her ears tuned for the sound of Ben's retreat.

The moment the rustle of his footsteps faded into the distance, she spun to Temperance.

Her friend's brows were raised, and she crossed her arms over her chest. "I take it you know him?"

Heidi fought to keep a blush from rising up her face. She and Temperance were close, but she'd never spoken of Ben. He was a part of her past too painful to talk about. The trick now would be keeping T from realizing exactly how important they'd been to each other, once upon a time. Temperance had shared everything about her own past, the good and the painful. Her friend would be hurt if she realized how much Heidi had held back.

So Heidi dipped her chin. "He's Reverend Lane's son. I think he and his older sister had already left for the West when you came to work at my aunt's." She knew that timing for certain, in fact, but better to act casual. "He and his older sister came to serve as missionaries to the natives."

Temperance eyed her. "And you just happened to run into him in t'is big, wide country?" The way she spoke a *t* sound instead of a *th* didn't usually stand out to Heidi anymore, but her exaggerated words made the accent even stronger.

And she was right. Meeting Ben so soon did seem a bit too coincidental. In truth, she'd *hoped* to find Ben out here. Had even planned to make a few inquiries if they found people who spoke English. If she *had* been able to locate Ben, she'd intended to pin him down for answers. Why had he deserted her so abruptly? What had she done to drive him away?

But stumbling on him in the first week after they'd begun mapping the Marias? The notion seemed impossible.

Could Ben have been searching for her? No. Of course not. What a silly thought. He couldn't have known the Guild & Forest Company commissioned Philip to explore and map this river. And he certainly couldn't have known she'd be assisting her cousin. His shock had been obvious when he'd spotted her.

Temperance waited for a reply.

Heidi shrugged. "This river must be a good place for the natives to live. I imagine we'll find a number of them camping on its banks as we travel. Perhaps he didn't make it any farther than this before he found a group of people who wished to learn about God." There. That sounded a likely answer.

Temperance gave her a look that said her story needed a bit more work. But she turned to the grave. "What do you t'ink? Does Mr. Philip need more rocks, or will he be safe?"

Heidi reached for another handful of wildflowers. "I think he's well covered. Let's give him some decorations though."

The hour seemed to stretch as she tried to keep herself busy.

Cleaning up around their camp. Gathering firewood. Anything to distract her mind from the topics that tugged at her.

What was she going to do about Ben? Part of her longed to forget him. To go on with her work and leave him behind. Just as he'd done her.

But she'd hoped to find him on this journey so she could force him to explain his actions. They'd been in love—at least *she* had. Ben *said* he was. He'd been the first to speak the word even.

He'd never officially requested her hand in marriage, but they'd planned. They'd dreamed. She'd been almost certain that when he came back from that trip to Pennsylvania he would ask Uncle Martin for his blessing.

But then he'd started to pull away, little by little. Not coming around as often, seeming distant when they were together.

Still, she'd refused to let herself see what he was doing. His announcement that he was going west to be a missionary with Elise had shocked her. She had worked up the courage to ask if she could come along, a way to let him know she wanted to be part of those plans if only he would make her his wife.

But he shook his head, not meeting her gaze. His words still rang in her ears. *You deserve better than that, Heidi. You deserve better than me. Once I'm out of the way, you can find a better man.*

There was so much she'd wanted to say in response. Surely he saw the truth—they were perfect for each other. But even in her stupid love-blindness, she could see he'd made up his mind.

It wasn't the first time she'd not been good enough. It might not be the last, but she wouldn't lower herself to beg.

Nor would she let down her defenses now. She scooped up another log and added it to the load in her arms. They already had plenty of wood at camp, especially if they moved on tomorrow morning as her heart craved to do. But this was the only thing she could think of to pass the time.

"Miss Heidi." Temperance's voice called from beside Philip's grave.

She spun and dropped her load. T only called her *miss* when others were around. Ben must have returned with his sister.

Heidi brushed the dirt from her hands and skirt as she strode toward them. Temperance stood a little to the side as three others gathered around the mound of rocks. Ben she could easily recognize. Was that Elise wearing a leather dress? And a native man standing beside her?

Her pulse quickened. She'd been worried enough about meeting Elise, but a stranger from a different culture, one who might not even speak her language?

She forced her breathing to stay even and fixed a pleasant expression on her face.

As she approached, Ben stepped around the grave to come closer. "Heidi, you remember my sister, Elise. This is her husband, Goes Ahead."

Husband. As the shock of that news sank in, Elise moved past her brother and swept up to Heidi, gripping her elbows with an expression that seemed to combine sadness and pleasure. "Oh, Heidi. It's so, so wonderful to see you. But Philip..." The sadness won, and a sheen glimmered in her eyes. "I'm sorry." Her voice caught with those last words. Then she pulled Heidi into a hug.

At first, Heidi could barely move. She'd so rarely been embraced, definitely not back when she lived with her parents. And only occasionally after she moved in with Aunt Bertie and Uncle Martin at fifteen years of age. After Ben left, Temperance had become her closest friend. But they didn't hug. That would have looked odd since T was Aunt Bertie's housekeeper. Their friendship hadn't been a secret, but they tried not to be flagrant with it, since society frowned upon such relationships.

But Elise's grasp felt so warm and comforting, it was hard not to want to fall in. Heidi slowly raised her hands from their limp position, but just as she touched the other woman's back, Elise pulled away, moving her grip back to Heidi's arms.

Her eyes rimmed red and she sniffed. "I haven't seen Philip in years, but he was only a year ahead of me in school. He was always kind...and smart too." She gave Heidi's hands a squeeze, then glanced at Temperance. "Will you introduce me to your friend?"

Friend.

The word settled around her with a feeling of rightness. With this fresh start, she didn't have to introduce T as her maid. They could be on equal footing.

After making quick introductions between the two, Temperance curtsied, and Elise smiled. "It's a pleasure to meet you, Temperance. And this is my husband, Goes Ahead." She motioned to the brave. Then she cut a sideways grin toward Heidi. "As you can see, much has changed since we left Marcyville."

Heidi's stomach flipped as a new thought slipped in. If Elise had married one of the natives, had Ben done the same? Her gaze moved to him before she could stop it. Wouldn't he have retrieved his wife as Elise had brought her husband?

Maybe not if he was trying to soften the blow. Perhaps he felt that heaping another shock on top of losing her cousin would be too much for her to take in a single day.

She steeled herself with another layer of determination. If he was married, she wouldn't let her pain show.

Pulling away from Elise, she stepped toward Philip's grave. "Thank you all for coming to honor my cousin."

The others seemed to understand her wish to move forward with the service, and they gathered around the stones. Ben and Elise spoke kind words about Philip, and she had to fight the burn of tears. She managed to keep all from falling except one or two, and Temperance's solid presence at her side helped.

But as Ben spoke the final prayer, her mind drifted to what

must happen next.

She and Temperance would have to finish this mission alone. She couldn't turn back.

Could she? To what? She'd left everything behind.

When she'd convinced her aunt and uncle to let her and Temperance go with Philip, she told them they would no longer need to support her. They could be finished with her raising and financial upkeep.

She was twenty-two years old, after all, practically a spinster with very few prospects. But what were her options? She hadn't enough schooling to become a schoolteacher. It was unlikely a wealthy family would find her suitable as a governess. That left positions as housekeeper or maid, and the thought of taking on either of those options made her want to curl into a ball.

She could draw, though, and Philip had been letting her do the finishing work on his maps for nearly six months. She could take over the rest of the mapmaking in his stead now. Before leaving St. Louis, Philip purchased all the supplies they would need for this journey, so she wouldn't have to worry about how to provide for her and Temperance until they returned to the States. When she handed in the completed maps, she would receive the final payment from the G&F Company.

She could wait until then to figure out the next step in her life. Perhaps her work making maps on this expedition would speak for itself. Others might be eager to commission her, despite the fact she was a woman.

By the time Ben spoke his *amen*, she'd hardened her resolve. She and Temperance would finish this assignment. They would be careful in their travels and keep to themselves, skirting any native villages that lay in their path. They were both capable women, and they could make this work.

God, if You've ever cared about me at all, please help me make this work.

Elise was the first to break the silence that settled over the group. She turned to Heidi and Temperance. "You must come to the village and stay with us. We'll feed you, and you can sleep in one of the lodges, out of the weather. Where are your things? Do you have horses?" Her gaze shifted to the land around them, searching.

Heidi bit her lip. Hadn't she just decided they would avoid villages? But a glance at the sky showed dark, ominous clouds in the distance. She hadn't yet fully learned to read the weather, but they'd been rained on often enough to know the cold and miserable experience.

Perhaps since Ben and Elise were here, she and Temperance would be safe enough in this village. Just this once.

She flicked her gaze around the group, and she couldn't help but linger on Elise's husband.

He met her look steadily. "You would be an honored guest among my people."

The man spoke English remarkably well. And something about him—maybe the gentleness in his expression—eased her fears. Sure, he looked different than most men of her acquaintance. His black hair hung long and plaited in braids, and his leather clothing certainly had a different style than she was accustomed to. But both his tone and words spoke of kindness. Just because someone looked different didn't make them bad.

She'd been the different one far too many times in her life to make the same mistake toward others.

She managed a smile for the man. "Thank you."

"Good." Elise spoke again. "Our lodge is a bit crowded and noisy with the children, but Goes Ahead's parents have plenty of room, and I know they'll welcome you. They don't speak much English, but I think you'll find them delightful."

Heidi slid a look at Temperance in time to see her eyes widen. It seemed they were about to be houseguests of an elderly native couple who spoke a completely different language. What in the world had they gotten themselves into?

CHAPTER 3

*P*erhaps spending time alone with Heidi was a bad idea, but Ben couldn't escape it now.

He ambled beside her the next day as they strolled toward the river's edge. She'd been the one to request this walk, so he'd assumed she wanted a place they could talk alone. He'd taken her upstream from the village where they could have a bit of privacy.

Perhaps she had news from home. Or maybe she wanted to ask for help now that her cousin had passed. He had so many questions about why she was here. Surely there would be enough to say without delving into their shared past—specifically why he'd pulled away from her at the end.

Neither of them spoke, but someone had to break the impasse. They couldn't return to camp until she'd said what she needed to. He'd always loved being with Heidi, even walking in companionable silence. But when he'd returned from that trip to Pennsylvania and realized what danger he could bring on her, he'd avoided time alone with her as much as he could. It was then he'd stilled his heart against the pain of losing her.

But leaving her had been his only choice to keep her safe.

Hadn't it? Would it have been better for him to fight for her innocence? But fight against corrupt officials? They were being bribed—heftily—to force her entire family to pay for crimes. Had she committed any of them?

He slid a glance at Heidi. Everyone made mistakes, but he couldn't imagine her swindling families out of hard-earned coin. Not this woman who'd reported to their teacher any schoolwork mismarked in her favor. Heidi had always been honest, even when the truth worked against her. Perhaps she'd developed that trait because she'd seen corruption and how badly it could damage people. He couldn't believe she'd willingly gone along with the things he'd overheard.

Should he ask her now? No, better to leave that in the past. He'd made his decision back in Marcyville and done what he'd had to for her safety. Because of that, he'd damaged their relationship beyond repair. Hopefully she wouldn't choose this place, so far from their home, and this time, just after burying her cousin, to ask about it.

"So," he started, "you're a mapmaker now."

She didn't look at him but stared into the distance, beyond the river. "Philip's been training me since he moved back to Marcyville. We've been contracted to map the path of the Marias River into the mountains."

It was impossible to miss the sadness in her voice. Would it be better for her to talk about her cousin, or wait until she'd processed his death? Philip had passed little more than a day before.

"I hope you'll stay with us a while until you feel up to the journey back. I can accompany you as far as St. Louis. Will you be returning to Marcyville?" He couldn't travel with her all the way home, not without bringing danger to her again. But he could at least make sure she had safe passage that far.

She turned to him. " I'm not going home until those maps are complete."

16

He blinked as his mind struggled to make sense of the words. "Finish the commission? With whom? It's only you and Miss McDonough, right? You can't travel into the north country by yourselves." That land was fraught with the more dangerous tribes, especially Blackfoot.

And even if they managed to stay clear of human threat— which wasn't likely, especially as summer brought the prime hunting months—two women alone couldn't manage in this wilderness. Hadn't she learned anything from Philip's death?

But one look at the fire flashing in her eyes showed she'd deciphered his thoughts. Or at least what his reaction inferred about her abilities. Heidi had always been independent and rarely backed down from a challenge. It was one of the things he'd loved first about her, the dogged way she went after what she wanted. Like catching up with the others in her grade, even though she'd moved to Marcyville in the middle of the year. His simple offer to help her study for a test all those years ago had turned into a first-hand account of her determination to overcome her challenges.

And now, he had no doubt she would spend her very last breath to accomplish this work if she set her mind to it.

He had to talk her out of it. Surely this was grief speaking. Once she had time to absorb Philip's death, she would see reason. He just had to keep her from doing something foolish until then.

He gentled his voice. "I hope you'll stay with us a while though. If you aren't comfortable with He Who Speaks Loud and his wife, I could stay with them. You and Temperance can take my place in Elise's lodge. With little Pretty Shield and Walking Bird there, the place can be noisy sometimes, but you might prefer to be around people you know. It's up to you. We just want you to feel comfortable."

She tipped her head, curiosity touching her gaze. "What's the story with them anyway? It doesn't seem like you've been gone long enough for her to have a son that old."

There was a hint of the old Heidi, the curious girl he could speak freely with.

"They were Goes Ahead's children with his first wife. She died in a massacre just before we met him. We helped him bring the children across the Rockies to this village where his parents live. He became a Christian on that journey, and the more he and Elise got to know each other..."

He shrugged. "I wasn't sure it was wise, bringing together two people from such different backgrounds, but God gave me a peace about their joining. He showed me this was His will, that He'd orchestrated their meeting for His purposes." Ben couldn't help but grin. "Elise loves the children. She's a natural mother, as you probably remember well." Elise had occasionally extended her mothering tendencies to Heidi when he brought her to the Lane home to study after school.

Heidi offered a wistful smile. "I've always liked your sister."

Then she turned toward the river and stared into the flowing water, and Ben tracked her gaze. The Marias wasn't as wide here as the Missouri, but a horse would likely have to swim across. If she attempted the trek upriver, she would have to cross the water several times. Did she know how to accomplish that safely?

He cut her a sideways look. "I assume you haven't learned to swim?"

She frowned at him. "No."

The lack of that skill alone could put her in real danger. And she'd face a host of other serious threats along the way. She'd never been exposed to a wild land like this. *He* wouldn't be eager to attempt the journey she intended without a guide, and he'd crossed the Rockies twice in the two and a half years he and Elise worked among the tribes in these towering mountains.

"Ben, what happened?" Her quiet words made him still, his chest seizing as his mind scrambled.

She meant between *them*. He couldn't tell her what he'd discovered, not without putting her in danger. He knew Heidi. The moment she returned to the States, she would march back to Westminton and confront those liars.

And it would be the death of her.

He couldn't allow that. Which meant he couldn't tell her.

He had to say something that wouldn't hurt her—not more than he'd already done. Something that would satisfy her but wouldn't give a hint of her danger. Without lying.

A tall order.

"I...um. Well, I just realized I'm not the right man for you. You deserve someone far better than me." His chest ached with even the idea that she belonged with another man. But he couldn't hold her back from happiness. He kept his gaze fixed on the water. He couldn't bear to see any pain that might flash in her eyes.

"Don't you think that's for me to decide?"

No. She would have chosen the path that put her in the most danger.

Before he could summon a response, she straightened. "I suppose it's in the past." She turned back the way they'd come. "Thank you for the offer of shelter, but Temperance and I plan to leave tomorrow morning. We have a lot of ground to cover before winter."

As she marched back toward the village, the set of her shoulders showed she wouldn't be swayed.

If he'd told her the truth, would she have stayed, at least a little longer? But he couldn't tell her.

That didn't stop the weight pressing so hard on his chest he could barely breathe. What should he do?

God, I've saved her from one threat to her life, but now she has an entirely different danger to face.

~

*H*eidi clenched her jaw as she marched back to the village. She couldn't think about Ben's words or she would succumb to the burning in her eyes. He still wouldn't tell her the truth. That much was obvious.

Or was it? Maybe what he said *had* been the truth, and she simply couldn't face it. Perhaps he never really loved her to begin with.

No. Of that much, she was certain. They'd both loved deeply.

How could he have changed his mind? Without even talking to her about his reasons. He was a better man than that.

Was there another woman? She couldn't let that thought consume her. She'd never be able to keep the tears at bay if she followed that trail. Besides, if he'd changed his affections to someone else, wouldn't he be with her now? There'd not been a young woman in the village he'd shown special preference to today.

As she approached the outer edge of the lodges, she could just see a gathering on the opposite side. At least three people mounted on horses. Was someone leaving? Or returning?

The woman Ben abandoned her for? She shoved that wayward thought aside and marched toward the group.

Others were stepping from lodges to see the commotion, and she eased her stride so she didn't run into anyone. As she neared the crowd, she could better make out the figures on horseback.

There were three, as she'd first thought. A white woman, a native man with something strapped on his back, and another man who appeared to be white, though it was hard to tell from this distance.

The woman dismounted first, and Elise stepped toward her and drew her into an embrace.

The action spurred a memory. On their long walk to the

village the day before, hadn't Elise said they were working as missionaries in this village with another man and woman? A white woman who'd married a man from the Shoshone tribe. The couple had gone to visit his family.

"Lola and White Owl have returned." Ben's voice rumbled from just behind her. "That's their daughter strapped to White Owl's back. I'm not sure who the other man is." He stepped beside her and gave a smile that reminded her too much of her old friend. "Shall we go see?"

She followed him as they wove through the crowd to where the new woman spoke to Elise.

Both ladies turned to her and Ben as they approached, and Lola gave Heidi a tentative smile. "Hello."

"We've had a bit of excitement too." Elise jumped in. "A good friend from back home arrived. Heidi Wallace, please allow me to introduce our friends and comrades, Lola and White Owl, and their sweet daughter, Anna. And this is Louis Charpentier, another friend who was staying with White Owl's family. I think he was ready to get out and see more of the country, so he agreed to come visit for a while."

Someone else stepped beside her, and she glanced over at Temperance. Reaching for her friend's arm, Heidi tugged her forward a little. "And this is my friend and traveling companion, Temperance McDonough."

T dipped in a quick curtsy, but Heidi tugged her back up. As far as she was concerned, Temperance was no longer in service. She might have come on this trip under the guise of acting as Heidi's lady's maid, but with Philip gone, she needed a friend far more than a paid companion. Besides, she wasn't actually being paid. They were both sharing the food and supplies, which put them on equal footing.

"How wonderful to have visitors." Lola smiled at them both, then glanced back at her husband. "Anna is asleep, so we'll unload and get settled in."

Lola and White Owl greeted a number of natives by name as they untied bundles from behind their saddles. Some of the young men took the horses, and the three newcomers wove their way through the crowd. White Owl led, Lola close behind. Louis followed, nodding at Heidi and Temperance when he passed them.

Was it her imagination, or did his gaze linger on T? Her curly red hair sometimes drew extra attention, and from the way Mr. Charpentier's mouth tipped upward, he must have found what he saw pleasing.

She studied him more closely as he walked away. He couldn't be more than twenty years old, with skin as sun-darkened as Ben's from dwelling outdoors. Had he always lived in this land? What brought him to the Shoshone village, and why had he left it now? His surname proclaimed him to be of French descent as surely as Temperance's stated loudly that she was Scotch-Irish.

Perhaps nothing would come of that look, nor of the way T gazed after him. She'd never truly been in love, as far as Heidi knew. Though she'd certainly admired a fair number of fellows. Each had eventually fallen below her standards, for though Temperance freely admired a handsome face, she'd spent enough time in service to know how she wanted to be regarded by the man she would give her heart to.

If only Heidi had been more careful in that area. At first, Ben had treated her better than any person ever had. Until he'd changed his mind.

The crowd had mostly dispersed, so Heidi turned to Temperance, who raised her brows, as though she knew what was coming.

Heidi squared her shoulders. "We're leaving tomorrow morning. Can we have things packed tonight so we'll be able to saddle the horses at first light?"

T's gaze turned worried. "We can, but are you certain?"

Heidi gave a firm nod. "Positively. We have too much to do. We can't waste even a day."

"I'll be ready t'en."

Maybe it was the quiet tone of her friend's voice that made her pause. Or maybe her own guilty conscience. Was she dishonoring Philip's memory to leave him behind so soon?

Once more, she shook off the thought that might slow her down. She couldn't afford distractions. Accomplishing this assignment and returning home safely would take every bit of her focus.

CHAPTER 4

"*S*he won't change her mind."

Ben's body recoiled from his sister's words as if they'd been the blast of a rifle. He'd prayed Elise would get through to the stubborn woman. He'd been pacing the dirt inside her lodge with Goes Ahead while their children slept, ever since his walk with Heidi earlier. Now, Elise had returned from trying to convince Heidi and Temperance to stay longer—to no avail.

Elise gave him a sad smile. "She's really determined, Ben. Nothing I said gave her pause at all. I think the more I talked, the stronger her determination grew." She let out a sigh and turned toward the cook fire. "We're going to have to let them go."

A surge of frustration whipped through him. "No."

She turned back, her face a question.

He shook his head hard. "I can't allow it. They'll never make it alone."

Elise glanced at her husband, who sat on the couch of buffalo hides, working with an arrow and some kind of metal rod. Goes Ahead met his wife's gaze, but it was impossible to tell the silent conversation that passed between them.

Elise must have understood, though, for she turned back to him with a hint of frustration in her tone. "What do you mean, you can't allow it?"

He straightened, his mind spinning through the specifics of what he'd just committed to. "I guess I'll be leaving at first light."

"Leaving for where?" Lola stepped inside the lodge, Anna on her hip with White Owl and Louis trailing behind. Ben hadn't had a chance to do more than introduce himself to the younger man, but the fellow possessed a pleasant expression that made a person like him immediately.

Elise's shoulders drooped as she turned to her friend. "He wants to go with Heidi and Temperance when they leave in the morning."

White Owl turned to Ben. "Where do they go?"

"They've been hired to travel up the Marias River, drawing maps of its path into the mountains."

Lola's eyes widened. "You're going with them the entire way?"

He braced his hands at his waist. "As far as they go. I won't let two young ladies ride off into the wilderness alone. Especially not Heidi."

Elise gave him a sympathetic look. He'd never told her his reasons for leaving Heidi behind, and thankfully, she'd never asked. But she knew how much he loved her. And she likely noticed his melancholy in those early months after they left Marcyville. He'd gotten better at hiding it after a while, though his feelings hadn't changed.

White Owl nodded, and the concerned look that passed between him and Lola showed they clearly understood his worries.

"Would it help to have another fellow along?" Louis stepped into the conversation. "I don't have anything tying me down right now, and I've been hankering for some travel." He flashed a grin. "If you're going north, you'll be headed back toward my homeland, though we came from the northeast, and I think the Marias flows from the northwest. Still, I'm happy to do what I can to keep the women safe."

That could be the perfect solution. Two men might not be much to protect the women from a Blackfoot war party, but at least he wouldn't be in it alone. "I'd be glad to have you along."

"You need someone who can speak the hand talk." White Owl made the sign *speak*. He shot a look toward Goes Ahead. "If you do not need me before winter, I can ride with these." He motioned to Ben.

"We'll both come," Lola spoke up. "The women might need protecting from you men." She shot a teasing grin from Ben to Louis.

Something in Ben's chest rose up, a feeling too much like hope. With all of them traveling together, they had a much better chance to survive the journey unharmed. He could help Heidi accomplish her work. And he wouldn't have to let her go again so soon.

They'd have an entire summer together. The thought of saying goodbye after that was more than he could stomach. Or maybe he could convince her to stay with him here, forever. For now, he would simply focus on keeping her safe and making it possible for her to do this work she was determined to carry out.

He glanced around the group, then slid a look to Elise and Goes Ahead. "Do you two want to come as well?"

Elise shook her head, a soft smile curving her mouth. "Our place is here right now, and it sounds like you have plenty of support. We'll pray for your safety every day you're gone."

He turned to the others. "Can you be ready to leave at first light? I could ask Heidi to delay a day if we need to." But whether she'd agree to that was uncertain.

Lola glanced at her husband. "We'll go pack now."

~

*T*his day had gone nothing at all like she'd planned.

Heidi hunkered beneath the crude parasol Ben had created with an oilcloth and a forked stick to keep her sketchbook dry as she worked. At least the rain had settled to a steady drizzle, not the sheets that fell when the downpour first started.

They'd set out this morning later than she intended—seven of them instead of just her and Temperance. The group included a baby who would surely slow them down, though Anna was a precious, chubby-cheeked cherub who possessed a remarkably happy temperament and a shock of black hair like her father's.

They'd been able to travel steadily enough through the first half of the day, but after the noon break to rest the horses, the sky had darkened and the rain had begun in strong pelts.

Thankfully, Philip had built a special waterproof case for the larger maps, so there was no danger those would get wet. Heidi simply had to protect this sketchbook she used as they rode, making preliminary drawings and notes she would use to create the final versions tonight. This was the part Philip had done, but she'd studied every one of his early sketches thoroughly as she used them to create the final renderings, so surely she could do this first step as well.

But the low dark clouds and the falling rain made it harder to see the detail of the land ahead.

The others waited patiently on horseback while she marked out the line of the little creek that fed into the Marias, as well as the approximate height of the bluffs on either side. Her companions were likely more miserable than she, for in addition to being soaked through, they had nothing to occupy them

27

as they waited, streams of water flowing off the hats of those who wore them and down the faces of those who didn't.

At least little Anna was staying mostly dry. White Owl had made the same kind of parasol canopy for his daughter that Heidi was using to protect her work.

Finally, she studied what she'd drawn to make sure she hadn't missed anything, lifted her gaze to the land around them to check, then closed the book and fastened the leather flap. She wrapped it in oilcloth, then slipped the bundle into the leather pouch and tucked it into her pack under one of the blankets. It was impossible to keep it completely dry, for dampness in the air seeped into everything, but that should secure the book for now.

She nodded to her fellow travelers, then nudged her gelding forward. The animal obeyed, stepping through the tall grass with his head ducked against the rain. The others started forward too, and the steady patter of drops grew faster, thickening the air around them. She shrank tighter into the oilskin she'd covered herself with and pulled the cover closer to her head, but it did little to protect her as the wind began blowing the rain sideways.

They rode for another half hour at least, around a wide curve in the river and through another tree-lined creek that fed into the main waterway. She needed to stop again and sketch what they'd passed before she forgot the details. But with the rain gusting all directions, the Y-shaped shelter above her wouldn't keep her sketchbook dry.

Maybe if she dismounted and moved under one of the trees.

She raised her arm to signal a halt, then pulled the bundle of books and her charcoal pencil from the pack, tucking them inside the flap of her coat.

Ben rode his horse close to hers, and she turned to see what he needed. He had to raise his voice to be heard over the pounding rain. "This tree cover might be a good place to stop for the night." He motioned toward the low branches lining the creek.

She eyed the sky. The gray clouds and rain made it impossible to tell how late the afternoon had grown. "We should push farther if we can."

He studied the land in front of them. They could barely see the winding of the river in the distance. "There're no trees as far as I can see. We need them to build a shelter large enough to keep everyone dry." He turned back to her. "You said you'll work on the large detailed maps tonight, right? You'll need a dry space for that and enough time with good lighting."

He was right about those needs, but how she would manage to keep the pages dry she wasn't sure. Yet she had to work on the final drawings while the landscape was fresh in her mind. She wasn't seasoned enough at this work to risk waiting.

So she nodded. Maybe it was best to have a shorter day this first time out. As a shiver worked through her, she couldn't deny a longing for a warm fire to dry her drenched clothing. That might be too much to hope for though.

As they rode toward the trees, she couldn't hear the words the men spoke behind her, but they seemed to agree on one particular section for camp. She dismounted along with the others, resting her Y-shaped cover on her shoulder like a parasol as she fumbled with cold fingers to unstrap her packs from the saddle.

"Get what ye need, and I'll bring t'e rest after I unsaddle t'e horses," Temperance called.

Philip had taken care of the animals while Heidi and Temperance set up camp, but they would have to establish a new order of things, and it would likely look different with so many here.

She glanced at the others, most of them also unfastening saddle packs. "Let's just unload and see what needs done next."

Ben pointed to the base of one of the wider trunks in the area. "Lay all supplies here until we get a cover up."

As she and Temperance worked to remove the bundles from their saddle horses first, then their two packhorses, Ben came to help them, appearing on the other side of the gelding she was unloading. This had been Philip's mount, but the horse could carry supplies instead of a rider now.

With rain running down her face and dripping from her eyelashes, she didn't have the energy to frown at Ben—she and Temperance were capable of seeing to their own work and didn't need him hovering—but she did lift her voice over the rain. "We'll take care of our own."

He shook his head. "I'm done with mine."

A glance over her shoulder showed his horse stood relieved of all burdens, even the saddle. Louis had come to help Temperance, so Heidi might as well give up her argument.

When they had the horses unsaddled, White Owl moved to take their reins. He'd already walked all the other animals out to the grassy area.

She waved him away. "We'll hobble them to graze. Help your wife."

"Let him take care of the animals, Heidi," Lola called from where she sat with the supplies and her sleeping daughter. "Come take cover with me while the men set up shelter for us."

Heidi held in a huff. Why did everyone think her incapable?

White Owl reached for the reins again, and she handed them over. If he wanted the task so badly, he could have it. There was certainly plenty to do at the camp.

Ben and Louis were already stretching large furs over an area of barren ground. Just having the protection of the trees helped keep much of the rain off. They wouldn't be able to make a shelter large enough for all of them to sleep in, but if she could just have a space to work on the maps for an hour or two, she could spend the night with a bit of dripping.

But by the time she and Temperance returned to camp with their third armload of wood, all three of the men were finishing the shelter, and it encompassed an area even larger than one of the biggest lodges back in their village. How had they brought so many furs and oilskins?

Lola had laid her sleeping daughter on a blanket and was setting out the dry wood they carried in their packs to start the fire. Hopefully these wet logs she and Temperance gathered could dry beside the heat of the blaze.

With all of them working together to make camp, they completed the task in what felt like minutes. She and Temperance would have spent hours strapping together shelter and trying to get a fire lit with the air so damp. And food. Lola had a delicious stew simmering by the time Heidi prepared a place dry enough to work on the map. She needed to get this part done while she still had daylight.

When Temperance brought her a bowl of steaming soup, she gave her friend a smile, which came far easier than she would have expected. "Thank you."

T winked. "'Tis not so terrible having traveling companions, is it now?"

Heidi offered a grimace. "I suppose not."

CHAPTER 5

*T*hank *You, God, for sunshine.* Ben lifted his face to the glorious rays and soaked in the warmth.

Yesterday's constant downpour had been the most miserable drenching he'd experienced in years.

"I think that's good enough for now."

Heidi's voice pulled him from the reverie, and he opened his eyes.

She was wrapping the book back in its oilcloth. One thing for certain, she took a great deal of care with her maps. A good thing, too, for she spent considerable effort on them. They were the purpose of this trip, after all.

Once she had the book tucked safely away, they started riding again—just the three of them this time—Heidi, Temperance, and him.

It had been easy enough to see yesterday that these long pauses while Heidi sketched were hard on little Anna. Being still in the saddle all day was challenging enough for the babe. But not having the horse's steady movements to soothe her made it difficult to keep the child occupied, especially in the rain.

The others had agreed it might be best to split into two

groups, so White Owl, Lola, Anna, and Louis rode ahead. After they traveled a couple hours, they would stop, let the horses graze, and allow Anna to crawl about while they waited for Heidi, Temperance, and him to catch up and move past them.

Ben had actually planned for only one person to stay with Heidi, and he'd feel safest if it was him, but Temperance had refused to leave her side.

He slid a glance toward the red-haired woman. She was a bit hard to read. Quiet when in the group, almost like a servant would be. Something about her manner didn't hint that she'd be bent toward shyness, though. Her meekness felt more like training, as if she were holding back.

Temperance didn't act that way with Heidi though. He'd seen how she spoke plainly when the two of them were alone. That made him like the woman even more. Anyone who'd connected that well with Heidi had to be someone he'd get along with too.

Their horses started up a bluff that concealed the river beside them. As they climbed, he leaned forward to help his mare in her efforts.

"What's t'at?" Temperance had already topped the hill and stared out over the water.

He nudged his mare faster, and they crested the hill just as Heidi sucked in a breath. "Is he...alive?"

It only took a heartbeat to find what they'd seen.

A body. Floating down the river.

But...face up?

He cupped his hands around his mouth and called, "Halloo there."

The figure jerked, then splashed as the man scrambled upright. The weight on Ben's chest eased. He was alive then, just...floating?

The fellow waved toward them, then called out across the distance. "Hello."

"It's Louis." Heidi's voice brightened with the same relief he was feeling. "I guess he decided to enjoy a swim now that the weather's warmer."

As if to prove her right, the man dipped below the water. A moment later, he resurfaced downstream, closer to their side of the river.

He waved at them again, and even though they weren't close enough to see his expression, his grin was easy to imagine. Louis possessed an easy smile you couldn't help but respond to.

Heidi returned the wave, then nudged her horse forward. They did need to keep moving. Did Louis plan to meet them at the water's edge, then walk barefoot back to where he'd left his horse?

Ben shook his head. The man could ride double with him.

"Is he still underwater?" The worry in Temperance's voice jerked his attention back to the river.

"He seems like a good swimmer. Maybe he's seeing how long he can hold his breath." But Heidi didn't sound convinced.

Temperance plunged her heels into her mount's sides, and the animal surged forward, dragging the packhorse behind. They ran down the slope toward the water.

Ben urged his own mare forward, as did Heidi. Like Temperance's, Heidi's packhorse slowed her. He'd asked if he could take over the animal so Heidi could focus better on her drawings, but of course she'd refused. Stubborn woman.

He pushed his mare faster to catch Temperance. Louis still hadn't surfaced in the river. Something must be wrong.

Temperance slowed her animals and turned to enter the water farther downstream than Ben had planned to.

He jerked hard on his mare's reins. "Do you see him?" The river was too murky for him to spot anything under the surface.

She didn't answer, just kicked her horse hard to enter the flow. The animal plunged in, the packhorse following obediently.

Ben scanned upstream and down. Nothing.

Lord, help us find him. Louis had been underwater far too long now. Had he surfaced and they hadn't spotted him?

Heidi reined her mount in at Ben's side. "Do you see him?"

"I don't think he would be this far downriver yet."

She lifted her voice. "Do you see him, T?"

A few seconds passed as Temperance studied the water, her horses wading deeper. The animals would have to swim soon.

"T'ere he is," Temperance shouted as she scrambled off her saddle and plunged into the flow. She must have seen him beneath the surface, for Louis's head hadn't popped up.

She would need help. "Stay here." Ben nudged his own mare forward. Heidi didn't swim, so surely she would stay ashore.

He pushed his horse hard to reach where Temperance had disappeared under the surface, but the current was too strong and deep for the mare to move quickly.

How much longer could Louis survive?

Lord, keep him alive. Let us get him out.

They couldn't lose anyone on this journey, especially not so soon. And from something so innocent as a carefree swim. Had he hit his head? Or maybe he'd caught on a root.

When Ben nearly reached Temperance's horses, her head bobbed above the water. She sucked in a breath. "I need a knife. He's stuck."

"Here." Ben grappled for the blade he kept sheathed at his waist.

Temperance sucked in breaths as he finally freed the tool. "Hurry! I'm not sure he's still alive." The panic in her voice matched the dread thundering in his chest.

He had to help. "I'll come down and cut him loose." He pushed off his saddle into the cold water.

"No!" Temperance gave a vehement shake of her head. "I know what to cut. Give it to me."

At her forceful insistence, he held out the knife to her, and she grabbed the handle, then plunged underwater. He sucked in a breath and dipped under, too, so he could follow her down. They didn't need two people stuck in whatever debris hid below.

Ben usually swam with his eyes closed, but he forced them open as he strained to see where Temperance swam. Beneath the surface, the water wasn't as murky as it had looked from above. Where was she?

His lungs tightened in the cool water, but he held his breath and continued his scan. There. He could just make out the floating form of Louis. He sat on the river's bottom, arms and legs drifting with the pull of the current. Something kept him secured at the waist.

Ben lifted his head for another gulp of air, then swam hard toward him. Temperance already sawed with the knife at whatever restrained him. Maybe a root or vine.

As he reached Louis, he grabbed hold of the man's shirt to keep himself from floating away. At that moment, Temperance must have finally cut him loose, for Louis pulled free and floated upward.

Ben reversed direction and grabbed Louis's arm, then swam as hard as he could toward the surface.

Temperance grabbed his other, and they finally burst into the air.

Ben sucked in a gulp of fresh breath as he turned to make sure Louis's mouth had come above the water. The man's head lulled to the side, his mouth open. As Ben moved, Louis's jaw dipped below the water. Ben jerked him up again.

Louis gave no response. No sign of breathing. No life at all.
Lord, please save him.

Heart pounding, Ben swam hard toward his mare, still planted in the river where he'd left her.

Temperance clutched Louis on the other side and was also swimming toward the animal, her jaw set hard with determination. Her own horses had moved back to shallower water, so getting Louis up on Ben's mare would be the quickest way to carry him back to land.

Don't let it be too late. How long had Louis been underwater? Five minutes? Maybe less. Thank God, Temperance had reacted so quickly, even before Ben realized Louis was in trouble.

When he reached his horse, he climbed aboard first, then pulled Louis up in front of him. With his upper body out of the water, the man flopped forward as much as Ben's grip around his belly would allow him.

Ben pulled hard on the reins and kicked his horse toward shore. Heidi had already dismounted and stood with her two horses and Temperance's.

Temperance. He shouldn't leave her in the water. But when he glanced back to see if he should slow down for her, she was already standing at waist high.

"Go." She waved him forward. "Get him to land."

He obeyed, plunging his heels into the mare's sides to urge her the rest of the way.

As soon as they climbed onto the bank, Heidi reached his side, and Ben slid from the horse, easing Louis down after him. He laid the lifeless man in the grass, his face taking on a frightening bluish tone.

"Is he...dead?" Heidi's voice broke as she dropped to her knees on Louis's other side.

"I don't know." Ben pressed his fingers against the cold neck, but his own heart was thundering too loud and his breaths too heavy to tell if there was a pulse. "You try."

He pulled his hand away, and Heidi placed her fingers in the spot. Ben tried to focus on the man's chest to see if he breathed or not.

He couldn't see any rise or fall, and Louis's face was a purplish white.

God, please. We need a miracle.

He needed to pray aloud.

Placing one hand on Louis's forehead and another on his shoulder, he dug deep to find that place of connection with the Lord. "Father, we need Your healing touch now. Breathe life into Louis. Fill his lungs with Your breath. Make his body work as You created it to."

He hovered a moment in that powerful presence of God. The sensation of being wrapped in His power.

"Lord, fill him with strength. Use Your presence to raise Louis's body up."

"Amen." Temperance had taken Heidi's spot at Louis's shoulder, with Heidi moving down to his legs. "We've got to roll him over so we can pound out t'e river water."

She gripped beneath his shoulder and struggled to lift and roll him. Ben hurried to help, and they rolled him to his side.

Temperance thumped her palm on Louis's back, speaking in a voice rich with feeling. "Ye've got to live. Rise up just like t'ose dry bones Ezekiel saw."

As though Louis had been sleeping and her words awakened him, his eyelids flickered, then parted, opening halfway.

As if the effort unlocked a dam, he turned his head to the side and rolled his body as a convulsion shook his shoulders. Water spewed from deep within him.

CHAPTER 6

*B*en sprang back just in time to miss a full shower of river water from Louis's gut, though he did get some of the spray. His clothes were soaked enough it made no difference.

While Louis heaved out the contents of his belly, Temperance spoke quietly to Heidi, who walked to the horses, hopefully to get a blanket to cover the man. Though the sun had been warm enough when they were dry, Louis's clammy skin now felt like ice.

After a few more excruciating minutes, Louis's spasms quieted, and he dropped back to the ground, still lying on his side as though he didn't have the energy to flop onto his back.

He took in a breath, then released it with a tiny cough.

"T'ere now." Temperance eased him to his back, and once more, Ben assisted. "T'ank You, Jesus."

Amen, Lord.

Louis's gaze locked on Temperance, and she reached for his hand, grasping it securely. Neither of them spoke.

Had Louis suffered severe injury? They needed to know his condition so they could treat him.

Ben touched the man's shoulder. "How do you feel?"

Louis gave a slow blink, as though sorting through his body parts for an answer. Then his gaze moved to Ben. "All right, I guess." His whisper rasped.

Temperance stroked the damp hair from his temple and cheek. "T'ere now. Ye'll be feelin' like yourself soon enough."

Heidi returned with her bedding, untying the leather strap as she dropped to her knees. "These should help warm you."

Louis finally turned on his back, a groan slipping out with the effort.

Heidi unfolded the blankets, and they spread two over his body. Now the man trembled, maybe as much from the cold as the shock of all he'd endured.

Ben pulled back while Temperance fussed with the covers around Louis's shoulders. "Do you remember what happened?"

Louis's eyes turned distant. "I was floating down the river. Just about took a nap in the warm sunshine. When I realized I'd reached you folks, I started swimming toward the bank. Something caught my trousers..." His brow furrowed as his gravelly voice faded.

"Afraid t'ose pants are gonna need stitched." Temperance's voice had returned to its usual cadence. "'Twas easier to cut t'em than t'e root."

Louis's eyes were sharp, his brow still lined. He must not remember her sawing him free. He was likely unconscious by the time she reached him.

Ben nodded toward her. "Temperance was the first to realize you were in trouble. She rode her horse straight into the water, packhorse tagging along behind. Then she dove down and found where you were caught. She cut you loose."

Louis hadn't moved his gaze from her. His throat worked before he spoke. "I suppose I owe you my life then."

"Her and the Lord above." Maybe Ben shouldn't have interrupted the connection that seemed to be growing between the two of them. But it had been God's hand that brought Louis back to life, he had no doubt of that. And he would always do his best to give praise for God's marvelous acts, as the Psalmist instructed.

After another moment, Louis blinked, then looked around. He lifted his head and strained to sit up. "Guess I can't be lazy."

"Are you sure you're ready?" No need for the man to collapse. He'd seen a fellow suffer terribly after taking in water into the lungs.

"I want to try." Louis extended his right hand, so Ben grabbed his arm and pulled. Once in a sitting position, Louis gripped his head in his hands and squeezed his eyes shut. "Boy, that water can set a man's head to pounding."

"I've a powder to help with t'at." Temperance spoke to Louis first, then looked to Ben and Heidi. "Should we start a fire here to get him warm?"

Ben glanced at Heidi. She seemed as undecided as he was, but she turned to Louis. "White Owl and Lola are upriver still. Do you think you can sit on a horse long enough to reach them, or should we bring them back here?"

She must be as anxious to cover ground as he was. But if Louis needed longer to recover in this place, Ben could go alert the others.

"I can ride." The words came out almost in a grunt as he leaned forward to struggle up to his feet. The effort must have been harder than he expected, or maybe it made the pounding in his head worse, for he shifted onto his hands and knees, then paused.

Ben gripped his upper arm. "When you're ready, let me lift you up." Perhaps it would be wise to let Louis rest longer. The man had nearly died, after all. He could take an hour to collect himself before they hit the trail again.

"Let's give it a go now." Louis lifted his head again and sent a wink, though the exhausted lines on his face belied the good humor. "I'll take that help though. Wouldn't want to swoon in front of the ladies. Temperance might have to catch me this time."

Ben couldn't help a grin. Louis had been affable from the start, and he had a way of bringing humor and charm to lighten a tense situation.

"We sure wouldn't want that." Ben adjusted his hold and lifted as Louis pushed to his feet.

Once standing, Louis offered another weary attempt at a smile, though the tight line of his mouth proved he was fighting pain. Maybe dizziness too.

Ben moved his hold down to the man's elbow, but didn't release him. "You think you can climb aboard my mare? She's a steady girl and doesn't mind riding double."

"Let's do it."

While Heidi held the horse, Ben helped hoist Louis into the saddle. Temperance stood on the other side to aid where she could.

When he was seated, Louis gripped the front of the saddle, leaning forward far more than usual.

"I'm coming up behind you." Ben placed his foot in the stirrup and swung up, then settled himself where he could keep Louis from falling in case the dizziness overwhelmed him.

At last, he gave Heidi and Temperance a nod. "I think we're ready." At least he prayed they were.

≈

*W*hat a day. Heidi worked to steady the pencil in her hand after the fright they'd had. They'd come so close to losing another soul for this map. Was the effort worth the cost? Had all cartographers of new lands gone through such trials?

She penciled in the slope of the hill on her paper, then

glanced up to gauge the height of the cliff leading down to the water. It was taller than what she'd drawn.

She shifted back to the sketch and adjusted the line of the water below. Would that detail matter to the G&F Company? She'd read their commission papers enough to memorize them and had helped Philip with drawings for six months before they started west, then for the nearly two months it took to reach the Marias. But she'd had so little time working with Philip along this exact river. There were topographical details here she'd never experienced before. And she wasn't certain what would matter to those who would be using the map.

She had to do her very best. If only her very best weren't such slow work.

The others had stayed with Louis to rest during the noon meal, his pallor and cough still worrisome. Meanwhile, she'd spent the entire time retracing her steps and capturing details she'd not been able to sketch after Louis's near-drowning, then moving ahead to start on the next drawings.

With the land so flat, she could still see the rest of the group, though she would move out of sight as soon as she topped this hill. It appeared the others were mounting their horses to catch up with her anyway. She recognized Ben's muscular profile helping Louis into position. He'd aged nicely the past few years. His jaw more prominent, more masculine than she remembered.

She worked to still the fluttering butterflies that wanted to take flight in her middle. Enough about Ben.

Already, the sun had moved well past the noon mark. Had they even ridden five miles today? Perhaps, but not much more than that. Sure, Louis's river incident had slowed them, but only a little.

Her sketches delayed their progress far more than anything else, but she had to get these right. At this pace, it might be winter before they reached where the river entered the heart of the Rockies.

Bemoaning what she couldn't change wouldn't help her get the work done. She simply had to move faster. Draw quicker. And not be distracted. Especially by Ben.

She'd managed half the next picture by the time the group caught up with her. She motioned them forward, not lifting her focus from the line of the small creek that fed into the Marias. "You all go ahead. I'll catch up to you."

Temperance halted her horses at Heidi's side. "Do you mind if I ride on wit Louis? He's still not lookin' himself yet." She spoke in the quiet, respectful tone she used when others were around.

Heidi sent her a quick half-smile. "Of course." She must truly be concerned. Usually she wouldn't leave Heidi's side, but this was good. T's steady presence would help Louis recover in no time.

"I'll be here." Ben's voice sounded quietly on her other side, then he spoke louder to the rest of the group. "You all ride ahead and find a place to settle a while."

Alone with Ben. Heidi would have to work even harder to focus on her drawings instead of him.

She studied her sketch and made corrections as the others talked through plans. By the time she nudged her horse forward, White Owl, Lola, Louis, and Temperance had disappeared beyond a line of trees that bordered the river's edge.

Thankfully, Ben stayed quiet as he guided his horse beside her. Easier to forget him if he didn't speak.

At the next location, she halted her gelding and turned to a new page in the book. The river widened here, almost creating a basin. She had to make sure she captured its size and proportion correctly.

After more than an hour had passed, she'd completed two more pages of sketches, but they'd not caught up with the others yet. Ben waited patiently while she drew, but even the horses began to show their frustration with the lack of action.

As she turned to a clean page and prepared to sketch the serpentine of the river in front of them, Ben's voice broke into her thoughts.

"Would it help if I took a clean sheet of paper and rode ahead to start drawing the outline of the next section? Then you could come behind me and fill in what I miss."

She looked up at him, trying to gauge his reason for asking. Was he so impatient? "I'm sorry I'm moving so slowly, but I have to make sure there's enough detail for me to finish later."

He gave her that look that always eased the sting of her mistakes when he'd helped her study after school. "It's a wonder you're able to draw as fast as you are. But I don't like sitting here doing nothing while you're working so feverishly." He shrugged. "I'm not trained for mapmaking, but I could at least sketch out the main landmarks so there's less for you to do after."

In their school days, he'd possessed a talent for drawing people, even with chalk on a slate. It might be worth at least testing his skill now.

Temperance had tried to help draw the maps when they first started up the Missouri. Her lack of talent in that area had shown quickly, and not even her intense determination to learn the art had developed enough skill to be passable. No matter how much she tried, she simply had no sense of relative distance.

That had been a disappointment for T, and maybe that was why she worked so hard to make up for it in every other way around camp. So often, she still acted like a hired servant, not an equal friend, no matter how many times Heidi assured her otherwise.

Who knew? Maybe Ben would prove up to the task.

Heidi reached for the tether strap attached to the back of her saddle and pulled the packhorse forward. Once she'd extracted

Philip's sketchbook from the pack, she handed it and her spare pencil to Ben and worked to ignore his fingers grazing hers.

"Open to the first clean page, then draw the same scene I'm working on."

His brown eyes locked on her as she explained what to do, his nearness and attention already heating her skin.

She forced her attention to the job at hand. "We'll do a few like this so I can show you what's important to catch on this first draft and what I'm able to add in later."

"Yes, ma'am." His smile undid her.

This would be harder than she'd imagined. She had to keep reminding herself that Benjamin Lane had left her before and, no doubt, he'd do it again.

eidi studied Ben's drawing, doing her best to focus on the pencil marks instead of how close he stood as he looked over her shoulder to examine his sketch beside hers. The three he'd done yesterday afternoon had gotten progressively better. And now, this first attempt today captured even more detail than her own did.

She motioned to a part of the cliff bank on his paper. "This is good. You don't have to shade the whole slope on this first draft. Just one corner to show how dark it should be for the elevation and type of rock, then a line to show how far that texture extends. I can fill in the rest on the final drawing tonight."

He nodded. "Makes sense. I wasn't sure if I captured the angle of the slope correctly." As he leaned in to point at a line on the far side of his drawing, his arm brushed against hers.

She took a step away, handing his sketchbook back. "It looks fine to me. Plenty for me to go on when I do the final drawing." She turned to her horse and put her foot in the stirrup to mount. "Why don't we split up now. I'll take the next section, and you go on ahead to the one after. That way we can get twice as much done."

And she wouldn't have to spend nearly so much time in his presence.

He studied her as she mounted, as though he could see through her words. Even if he could, it didn't matter.

At last, he mounted his own horse. "Let's go then."

After moving to the next section, she pointed out the area she would draw, and he rode on to the portion beyond.

As she began to lay out the line of the river, Temperance waited quietly on her mare. Not many people could be as silent and patient as T.

But then her brogue shattered the peacefulness. "Ye know, not many men would work so hard to help out a friend as he is."

Perhaps Temperance didn't always stay as silent as Heidi would like.

She kept working. The last thing she wanted to do was discuss Ben's merits.

The lack of conversation didn't seem to bother T. "I suppose preachin' a funeral is somet'ing any man of God would do if asked. And it's common kindness to offer shelter to two women who stopped in for a visit. But it seems to me t'at droppin' everyt'ing he had to do and gatherin' up a group large enough for protection, t'en travelin' on with us for who knows how many months, is a mite more t'an most would do."

She slid Temperance a warning look, but her friend met it with raised brows.

"I'm not meanin' to be pushy, I just tink it bears noticin' what a good man he is."

Heidi did her best to focus on the drawing again. "I know he's a good man, but I have work to do." And the last thing she wanted to focus on was Ben's many good qualities. She had to keep in mind that one massive failing. The fact that he'd turned his back on her. Without so much as an explanation.

Even now, he still wouldn't give her the reason.

No matter how many good deeds he performed, no matter how helpful he was, she couldn't trust Ben Lane.

But though Temperance didn't speak of him so forthrightly again, just knowing her friend thought of Ben so kindly rubbed the raw edges of Heidi's nerves. Especially when they caught up with him and the others in a little meadow where they'd stopped for the midday meal.

She did her best to nod politely as Lola handed her something that looked like a sandwich made from a muffin. "Thank you. I'm going to walk to the river for a minute. I'll be back soon."

She turned and strode away before anyone could offer to accompany her. Maybe they'd think she needed to attend to personal matters.

In truth, she craved a quiet moment alone. Away from eyes that saw too much. Away from Ben's presence that stirred too many feelings. Away from the constant effort to maintain her defenses.

The river wasn't as wide here as in some places, and the bank was steep, but not a vertical cliff like downstream. She could grab on to the top edge and half-climb, half-slide down to where the land leveled out just before meeting the water.

Little animals had worn a trail in the dirt as they skittered along the river's edge. Would this be beavers? That was one of the prized furs that came from the West. And they lived by the water. But likely other creatures also used this path. She'd have to ask White Owl or Louis if they knew these tracks.

She followed the narrow path upstream, tucking her skirts so they didn't drift into the water. The wall of rock beside her had become even steeper, with a number of points jutting out in odd angles. What had made the stone form like this? It seemed that the river flowing through would have smoothed the walls, not left so many points.

One rock that jutted out from the cliff protruded into her

narrow pathway, and she had to grab hold of it as she arched her body over the water to move around without stepping into the river. She'd never learned to swim. Had never spent so much time around water in her life as since they'd first set sail up the Missouri to this place.

Though the river wouldn't be deep here at the edge, she would rather keep her shoes dry if she could.

On the other side of that protruding rock, an opening in the cliff wall snagged her notice. The gap wasn't as wide as her body and rose up half as tall as she was.

The inside of the small cave was dark and moved in at a slant. Could this be a deep tunnel? Or only a shallow animal burrow?

She bent to better see inside. Something within moved, and she jumped, her heart pounding as she tensed to back away.

But she made out a tiny form in the shadows. Some kind of tiny animal.

Another moved near the first one. Maybe this was a nest with babies. A tiny chirp-like sound echoed from inside. These were too large to be birds. Perhaps baby beavers? Or some other creature about that size.

The chirp sounded again. Her eyes had adjusted to the dimness enough that she could see the little creature move as it made the sound.

"Hello. Aren't you cute."

Her voice seemed to panic the animals, both scurrying closer together, chirping back at her.

She pulled away a little and lowered her voice to a whisper. "I'm sorry, I didn't mean to frighten you. I won't hurt you, I promise."

A light splash sounded behind her, and she glanced back as an animal bobbed up from the water, padding onto the ground behind her. The creature looked like the stuffed beavers she'd seen back in St. Louis, but...not quite.

It paused half out of the water and stared beady eyes at her, then opened its mouth and bared its teeth with a hiss.

She scrambled backward but smacked into the stone that protruded into the path.

The animal hissed again and advanced fully out of the water, opening its mouth wider to display what looked like fangs. Only one long stride separated it from her.

She squealed and scrambled around the rock. But the creature darted toward her, charging with those teeth bared.

She spun to run, but in her panic, her balance shifted too far over the water. She grabbed for the rock, but there was no place for her hands to find purchase.

For a suspended heartbeat, she hung there. Another hiss sounded from behind her. Was the creature still charging? Would it chase her into the river?

Her arm hit the water first, and cold plunged over her shoulder and neck. She fumbled for the river bottom to push herself up.

Thankfully the water was only as deep as the length of her arm. She craned to see if the animal was still coming.

It stood on the bank, nattering at her, those fangs still exposed as if daring her to step back into its territory.

Slowly, she gathered her feet underneath her, edging sideways, away from the critter.

"Heidi?" Ben's voice sounded from the bank above.

She wanted to cry out for help. To save her from this violent oversized rodent with knife-like fangs and pull her out of the dirty river water. She had no desire or energy to resurrect her frustration with him.

His head appeared over the edge of the cliff. "Heidi?" Something like panic laced his voice. "Hold on. I'm coming."

"I'm all right." She wasn't hurt, but she must look a sight, drenched and still crouched in the water.

He'd already started down the cliff wall, which thankfully wasn't much taller than Ben.

She forced herself up onto all fours as he landed on the narrow path.

"Let me help you." He grabbed her arm and helped her up.

"What is that thing?" She pointed to the animal peering around the rock. "I think it has babies in a den there. Two that I saw."

As Ben followed her gaze, he tugged her farther from the animal. "Muskrat, I think. She might attack if she thinks they're in danger."

She let Ben pull her to land, her boots squishing. "I'm a mess."

He started down the path, still holding her elbow as if he thought she might topple back into the water. "We can't seem to stay out of the river on this trip, can we?"

He glanced back at her, a smile playing at his mouth. "I'm just glad it wasn't deep there."

That made two of them.

She followed, letting him tug her as they went.

He stopped at a low boulder in the path. "I think we can make it up the bank here." He stepped onto the rock, and she followed.

She could just see over the top of the bank.

"I'll lift you up so you can climb over."

Holding her arm was bad enough, but she couldn't let him come close enough to hoist her. "We should go downriver where the bank's not so high."

But he had already placed his hands at her waist and was lifting, just like he used to help her into the back of his family's wagon when they picked her up on the way to church.

She braced her elbows on top of the bank and lifted one leg over. That gave her enough leverage to pull herself up. She rolled onto the grass, then scooted into a sitting position as Ben climbed up behind her.

They both sat for a moment, collecting themselves. A cluster of bushes hid the rest of the group from view. Had they heard her cry out? Why was Ben the only one who'd come? If Temperance thought she was in trouble, she would have been here posthaste.

"I was coming to check the horses when I heard you yell." An embarrassed look slipped over his face. "I wasn't trying to invade your privacy, I promise. I thought my horse was limping there at the end, and I wanted to check her hooves."

Ben wouldn't lie. He might withhold the truth, but his honesty was always one of the traits that drew her to him.

She lifted her sodden skirts. "I'm a wet mess. I guess I'll dry quick enough in the sun though."

As he looked at her skirts, humor glimmered in his eyes. But when his gaze scanned up to her face, it shifted into something...different.

Something far too much like admiration.

A weight pressed on her chest, and a burn surged to her eyes. She had to get away from him before her emotions rose too strong.

She pushed up to her feet. "I need to get back." She didn't give him time to respond.

As she strode toward the others, she blinked away the tears and searched hard for the shield she usually kept in place. Hadn't she moved past the point of crying over Ben? She couldn't let him get close enough to affect her again.

CHAPTER 8

*B*en squeezed his eyes shut to block out the sight of Heidi walking away from him.

Nay, *marching* away from him.

Everything in him wanted to reach out and take her in his arms. Had he made the wrong choice back in Marcyville? If only he could have begged Heidi to come with him and Elise when they first went west.

He'd not realized it before he'd come to this land, but this territory was so remote, she'd be safe from the men determined to find and kill her family. If she agreed to stay here with him now, they could make a life here. Together.

He'd have to tell her the truth about what he'd learned. If he did, would she agree to stay with him? Or had he hurt her so badly she would want nothing to do with him?

That seemed the most likely, given her actions on this trip.

He scrubbed his fingers through his hair, gripping the ends and tugging. The pain did nothing to vent his frustration.

God, what do I do here? How can I make this right? How can I get her to give me another chance?

No answer pressed in his spirit. No idea slipped into his mind as the Lord's directions often did. Nothing came clear.

Should I not try for another chance? Should I let her keep her distance and force myself to be content with only helping?

Still no sense of peace. The churning in his spirit didn't ease.

He groaned again and dropped his hands, turning toward the horses.

They'd hobbled the animals to graze while they ate, but his mare had shuffled a little away from the others. Hopefully the limp he'd detected was nothing. This was a new mount, which he'd traded for his other horse in Goes Ahead's village. He loved her sweet spirit and easy-going attitude. She'd been a pleasure on these first three days out.

Had it only been three days? It felt like a month since they'd left the Gros Ventre camp.

How was Elise doing? She surely had her hands full with her new family, but motherhood fit her perfectly. It always had. She was fifth in their family of twelve children but had been the second mother in the group that still lived at home during his growing up years. She'd put up with a lot from Ben, especially in his younger days. Hopefully Goes Ahead treasured her as much as she deserved. Ben didn't doubt it. She'd found a good man, one who loved her. But his brotherly instincts still rose up strong.

He reached the bay mare, and she lifted her head to greet him. He let her sniff his hand as he stroked the sleek hair at her neck. "How are you, girl? You enjoying the rest?"

She dropped her head to graze, and he ran his hand along her shoulder, then down the left front leg. This was the one she'd been limping on.

There was no heat in the limb that he could feel, so he unfastened the hobble to pick up the hoof. As she shifted her weight to allow him to lift the foot, the cause of her pain came immediately clear.

A gash ran from the soft spot at the back of her heel across the sole, through the center of the V flesh he'd once heard called a *frog*. "Oh, girl, no wonder you're hurting." The cut looked fairly fresh, with dirt darkening the blood that had clotted over it. She must have injured herself on the rocky section where he'd stopped to do his last sketch.

He studied the hoof. What should he do to help her heal? He'd never been good at nursing. Maybe he should wash the dirt and blood off. Then try to cover the wound? They could wrap the hoof in leather. Would she tolerate something tied around her ankle? Maybe he should ask Lola if she had a salve that would help. She and Elise had done all the doctoring during their travels.

He eased the mare's hoof down, then stroked her shoulder. "Let me see what we can do to help you."

She lifted her head around to give him a gentle nudge on his leg. Like a *thank you*.

"Good girl." He gave a final pat, then turned back to where the others waited.

As he strode to the group, White Owl stood off to the side, playing with his daughter. Lola, Heidi, and Temperance had gathered around the food, packing it up from the looks of things. Louis lay stretched out in the sunshine. All turned to him as he approached.

"Is she well?" Lola asked.

He braced his hands at his waist. "She's got a pretty deep gash on the bottom of her hoof. In that soft V."

Her brows lowered. "Is it bad enough it should be wrapped? Does she need to rest longer?"

"It's pretty dirty. I don't know if horse hooves fester like cuts in people do. It looks like it pains her."

Lola set aside her pack and rose. "I have a salve we can use. Maybe you can get a pan of water from the river to clean the hoof."

Heidi had barely glanced up at him, but Temperance frowned. "Is she too injured to go on? You could ride one of our packhorses if you think she can walk with us." Temperance looked to Heidi, maybe for agreement with what she offered.

Heidi offered a single nod. "Of course. Philip's horse would be the best. We'd have to rearrange the packs." She still didn't look at him, but addressed the words to Temperance.

He pushed down a spurt of frustration. He'd have to talk with Heidi later. Something had to change between them.

By the time he'd unpacked a pot and filled it with river water, Lola bent beside his mare, holding the hoof in both her hands as she studied the wound.

She took the pot from him and poured some of the water over the hoof. "It's a bad one. It should definitely be salved and wrapped."

"Can she keep going if I don't ride her?" What would he do if the horse needed rest? He couldn't stay behind, nor could he delay Heidi's work. She had to finish before winter set in. Should the mare be turned loose? Would she find her way back to the Gros Ventre village?

"I think she can handle that," Lola said. "We'll keep an eye on how much she limps."

Within a quarter hour, Lola had done a masterful job of tending the hoof and wrapping it in layers of thick buckskin. He'd switched his saddle to the big gelding that had been Philip's mount, and his sweet mare carried the pack saddle, relieved of as many bundles as he could fasten to the gelding.

As they started out, his new mount felt like a draft horse compared to the Indian pony. Philip had been a big man, with wide shoulders and a stocky build. His horse was the same, and perhaps the animal did have a bit of draft in his bloodline.

When they reached the first section that hadn't been sketched yet, Heidi reined in. "I'll start here. You go on to that bluff and draw the next area." Without looking at Ben, she motioned to a large boulder in the distance.

Temperance had halted beside her, and Louis also drew back on his reins. "If you ladies don't mind, I guess I'd like to hang back a bit with you. It might be nice to see the sights a little slower."

Louis's charm showed in the casual way he said the words and his hopeful grin. The man's goal was easy enough to see, though, at least for Ben. Ben had stayed back with Heidi and Temperance from the beginning to help if they ran into trouble. But since he was sketching on his own now, he would often be out of sight of the women. Louis was stepping in to take over as protector.

Ben should be grateful. He *was* grateful. And he forced himself to send a nod of thanks to the man.

But as he left Heidi behind and rode on with White Owl, Lola, and their daughter, he couldn't shake the prick of jealousy spearing his chest.

He wanted to be with Heidi, offering his protection should she need it. Sure he also wanted to relieve her of some of the immense task of mapping this land. To share that heavy burden.

But he'd also like to be *with* her.

He forced out a long breath. *Cleanse my heart, O God.* The Psalmist's words fit especially well just now.

When he reached the bluff, he waved farewell to White Owl and Lola and little Anna. They would ride on until midafternoon and look for a good place to camp for the night. Hopefully his help in drawing would speed up their travel and make the journey easier for all.

He halted the big gelding by a cluster of boulders and pulled out his sketchbook and pencil. From this elevated position, he could see several curves of the river. This type of landscape reminded him of the Missouri they'd traveled when they first came West.

As he finished drawing the outline of the river, the gelding beneath him jerked its head up. Ben reached for the reins. "Easy, boy."

The horse shuffled to the left, turning its head and perking its ears.

Ben stuffed the pad and pencil into the open pack and tightened his hold on the reins with one hand as he patted the animal's neck with his other. "What is it?"

A sound broke through his awareness, like the sizzle of water in a scalding hot frying pan. A tingle slid down his back as realization swept in.

A rattlesnake.

In the same heartbeat, his horse exploded.

The animal jerked sideways away from the snake. Ben clutched tight to the reins, but his legs didn't have a firm enough hold around the horse's sides to keep him moving with the animal.

He tipped sideways but clung to the leathers. The gelding shied frantically away from the snakes.

That awful rattle filled the air again as everything moved so slowly, yet so quickly.

Ben hit the ground, landing on his upper arm first, then his hip.

The horse jerked away, pulling him with the reins, spinning him around.

He lost his hold, and the animal leapt forward, sprinting and bucking in turns.

Ben lay in the dust and grass. His arm throbbed.

But then the rattle sounded again, and his mind scrambled into full awareness.

He had to get away. Wasn't this how Philip had died? Rattlesnake bite?

Panic clawed through him as he scrambled up to all fours. Pain shot up his arm, but he couldn't slow down.

CHAPTER 9

*B*en saw the rattlesnake from the corner of his eye, coiled in a thick circle, head and tail raised. Not more than three strides away. Was that close enough to strike?

He crouched on his hunches, preparing to fling backwards if he needed to. If he could move slowly enough not to threaten the animal, he had a better chance of getting away without a bite.

Easing up to standing a little at a time, he took a step back. Then another.

He didn't breathe, forcing himself to move slowly, fighting the frustration trying to claw its way up his throat. His pulse hammered through his body, but he'd backed four steps now.

Four small steps. Maybe he was out of striking distance.

A movement behind the snake caught his gaze.

More snakes. Three others coiled among the rocks. Had he stumbled on a nest of rattlers?

Just like Philip. And he'd been riding Philip's horse. Such a strange coincidence.

He would worry about that later. Right now, he had to get away from this place without getting bitten.

As he backed a few more steps, he slid his gaze to one side, then the other. Just to make sure he wasn't backing into another den.

No snakes on either side. At least not that he could see.

He eased back a few more steps. He had to be outside of striking range now. He turned and sprinted down the slope.

When he reached a more level area, he allowed himself to stop and breathe. His pulse still pounded hard in his neck, and his arm throbbed where he'd landed on it.

He gripped his elbow to help support the limb, but touching it sent the ache all the way through his shoulder. *Lord, please don't let it be broken.* He could move his fingers and the elbow joint. Surely that was a good sign.

The pain would go away soon. *Please, let it go away.*

In the meantime, he had to catch his gelding. Good thing he'd had the presence of mind to tuck his pad and pencil in the pack. If he'd dropped them, retrieving them from the middle of a rattlesnake den might be a greater challenge than even he was willing to face.

A glance around showed the gelding had meandered back the way they'd come. Ben's gut tightened. Heidi, Temperance, and Louis would have seen the mount running free.

It shouldn't bother him that they'd know he'd been thrown. After all, if there was ever a good reason, stumbling into a rattlesnake den surely counted.

But if he'd been paying better attention, maybe he would have seen the threat first. Or at least been able to stay atop the horse when it shied away.

I'm sorry for my pride, Lord. Help me focus on You and not what others think of me.

As he trudged toward the group, they moved his direction. Louis had grabbed his gelding's reins and was ponying the horse behind his mount.

As soon as they came near enough to be heard without shouting, Heidi called out, "Are you hurt?"

He was still gripping his elbow to hold up his aching arm, but he lowered his hand before answering. "Just a bruise or two." At least he hoped that was all it was. The pain in the arm seemed to be growing worse, not better.

"What happened?" Louis reached Ben and slid from his mount.

"Rattlesnakes." Ben started to take the gelding's reins, but the way Heidi gasped made him pause.

Her face blanched white, and Temperance clutched a hand to her throat. What had he been thinking, blurting out like that after Philip had died from the same thing days before? They might have even witnessed his attack. They'd surely watched his death.

Ben shook his head quickly. "I wasn't bitten." He gathered the horse's reins and rubbed the gelding's head. "This boy must have sensed them and started fidgeting. The moment we heard the first rattle, he bolted. I hit the ground, but far enough away I was able to move out of striking distance."

Heidi nodded, but the color didn't return to her face. They needed to put this episode behind them.

He moved to the gelding's side and tried to reach up to gather his reins. His left arm wouldn't lift though. As he tried harder, a searing pain stole his breath. And even when he tried to fight past the ache, the arm would only lift halfway.

He lowered the elbow back to his side and fought to keep moving, to reach up with his other hand and gather the reins, then grip the saddle.

As he slipped his foot in the stirrup and hauled himself onto the animal's back, he kept his injured arm pinned to his side. The world around him blurred.

Thankfully, Louis stood at the horse's head so the gelding stayed still. With the spinning in Ben's head, he might not have been able to stay aboard if the animal moved. He squeezed his eyes shut to see if that helped settle things.

It didn't.

He opened his eyes, and at last his view sharpened.

"You're hurt." Heidi's voice hadn't carried that much worry since back in Marcyville. For a heartbeat, he wanted to soak it in. To allow her to fuss over him.

But he couldn't let her fret. His pain or weakness shouldn't make things harder on her. He had to help, not hinder. It was the only way to win her good opinion again.

So he shook his head but caught himself after the first jerk sent flashes through his vision. He clenched his jaw and held his skull perfectly still so things would settle again. "Not hurt. Just need to work out the aches." He struggled for a grin. "I'm not as young as I used to be."

Her mouth formed a thin line that held no hint of a smile. "Can you ride up to Lola and White Owl? You should stay with them and have Lola check your arm."

He didn't attempt to shake his head again but added determination to his tone. "I'm fine. I'm going back to finish my drawing. I'll stay away from the snakes." Far, far away.

If anything, the tension in her features tightened even more. She glanced at the man still holding his horse. "Take Louis with you."

Ben met Louis's gaze and tried for another smile. It would be good to have his eyes and hands to keep a lookout for more snakes.

But hiding the pain in his arm from this man would be a challenge. At least it wasn't the arm he used to draw with.

*H*eidi straightened from the drawing and arched her back to loosen her muscles. Sketching by firelight always made her eyes ache and her shoulders tense, which was why she usually tried to finish the larger detailed drawing as soon as they stopped for the night, before dark settled in full.

But she'd been delayed this time. It wasn't until after they'd set up camp that Ben finally admitted how bad his arm was hurt. She'd suspected as much when he kept it close to his side all day.

The entire upper part of the arm just below his shoulder was swollen. White Owl said he'd seen such a thing before. It might be that the bone inside was broken, or maybe only weak. But the way to help it heal was to wrap a straight stick against it to strengthen the limb, then create a sling to hold the arm close to the body.

Heidi slid a glance at Ben. He'd been staring into the fire while she drew.

He didn't meet her gaze now. In fact, it almost seemed like he didn't realize she was there. With the others down by the river, this was the time to tell him what she and Temperance had decided.

Her mouth went dry at the thought of it, so she swallowed to revive some moisture. Could she really send him away? She had to. For his own safety, and that of the others.

She cleared her throat. "Ben." That word came out weak, so she strengthened her tone. "I think it's time you and the others go back. Temperance and I want to finish the work alone."

He jerked his head toward her, and pain flashed in his eyes. From the sudden movement or from what she'd said? "Why?"

She nodded toward his arm. "I don't want anyone else hurt. This isn't your fight. Temperance and I promised Philip that we would fulfill this commission." Her throat caught as an image of her cousin slipped through her mind. "He won't be with us, but we still aim to finish the work."

She glanced toward the river. The murmur of their friends' voices drifted to them. "It's not right to put the rest of you in danger. White Owl and Lola and that sweet little baby… They should be home building their life, not looking for ways to keep Anna occupied while they stand around and watch me draw."

Ben's brow lowered, and the shadows cast by the flame made him look angry. "White Owl will be a great help when we meet with natives."

She shook her head. "It's not worth the risk and hardship to them." She motioned to his arm. "You nearly died today, just like Philip. And even though you survived, your arm may well be broken."

"It's nothing, Heidi. Don't worry about me."

She wanted to shake him, but she forced her voice to remain level, her tone solid so he would know she meant every word. "Ben. I want you all to leave. In the morning."

He turned fully to face her, casting even more shadows across his expression. "Heidi." His voice came out soft. Gentle. "I left you once, and it was the biggest mistake of my life. I won't leave you again."

The words slammed into her, stealing her breath. Closing off her throat so no air would come in and no sound could slip out. The biggest mistake of his life? Did he really feel that way? Then…why?

She finally managed to squeeze out that single question. "Why did you leave me?"

Ben sat quietly. So still. If he gave that same old *I wasn't good enough for you* response, she would scream. Then stomp away. And maybe even pack up what belonged to her and Temperance and ride off into the night.

Maybe Ben realized that. He'd always had an uncanny knack for guessing her thoughts.

His voice came out even softer than before. "Do you remember when I took that trip to Pennsylvania to deliver Gretta to the school there?"

That long-familiar pain twisted in her middle. "Yes." She'd thought of him every second he was gone. And when he returned, he acted like he'd missed her every bit as much. At first.

" After I dropped Gretta off, I went to Westminton to find your father."

Once more, his words stole her breath, but this time in a very different way. Her father? Just that word clawed at her throat as panic welled up. "Why would you do that?" Her voice quivered, but she couldn't stop it. Had he learned the truth about her family?

Ben stayed quiet almost as long as before. She couldn't breathe. What did he know?

At last, he spoke in that same quiet tone. " I wanted to ask for his daughter's hand in marriage." He paused only long enough for his words to register in her numb mind before he hurried on. "Maybe I shouldn't have said that. Your aunt told me your parents still lived in Ohio, so I took the train to Marietta. When I arrived in Westminton, I rented a room at the boarding house. I didn't have your family's address, but it was a small enough town I thought I could ask around. The first few stores I stopped at, the people acted strange when I mentioned your family name, then every one of them said they didn't know a Mr. Wallace. The next shop was the mercantile."

She could only take in tiny gasps of air at a time. Walbert's Mercantile? Her family had cheated him out of so much money, even her twin sisters had swindled the man when they were so little they should have been innocent. The man had once vowed to see them all rot in prison.

The way Ben was studying her... Could he see her reaction?

She'd assumed the shadows made her expression as hard to read as his, but maybe not.

Yet if he already knew everything, why would it matter if she showed her panic?

When Ben finally spoke again, his voice turned serious. "I guess they didn't hear me come in. There wasn't a bell or anything over the door. I went to the counter, but before I could call out, I heard men talking in a back room. At first, I was just going to wait, but then I heard your name, Wallace. That's what made me listen, but it took me a while to figure out what they were saying. One of the men must have been a sheriff or judge, because at one point he said he was responsible for keeping order in that whole county, and he planned to see your entire family hang."

She stiffened, though it wasn't the first time she'd heard those words. Yet coming from Ben's mouth...

"Heidi, they said they'd given an enormous bribe to the governor, and he would be sending out a command to every town in the state to round up your family. They said they didn't know where you were, but they'd been looking for you for years and hadn't found you. I was so flabbergasted, I didn't think to get out of there before they realized I'd heard. The owner, a man named Walbert, came out and got as angry as a rooster in the hen house when he saw me there. He brought the other man out, and I realized he'd been in the leather shop where I'd asked about your family. He'd been watching me with a strange look, but never said anything to me there. Now, he knew that not only was I asking about your family, but I'd overheard every-thing he and Walbert said.

"I knew I had to get out of there. I couldn't let them know where I was from or let them follow me back to Marcyville. I tried to play like I knew the family from a long time ago and was just in town looking them up again. As soon as I got out of the store, I started walking. Out of town and up the main road between there and Marietta. When I got to the train station, I bought the first ticket east and stayed on until Pennsylvania. Then I borrowed a horse from the livery and rode south, where I finally took a train west to Marcyville."

Ben paused for a moment. Was he waiting for her to speak? She couldn't. Part of her had known she would have to tell him of her family's sins one day. But now that day had come, the dread clenching her insides stole her ability to form words.

"I didn't know what to do. I realized I'd given my name at the boardinghouse, but not where I was from. If they started searching wide enough, they might eventually find Ben Lane of Marcyville. But since your last name is different from your aunt and uncle's, I thought it would be a lot harder for them to track down a woman.

"It wasn't until I saw you again that I came to terms with what I had to do. My presence put you in danger. When Elise came up with this idea to go west and be missionaries to the natives, it felt like God giving me the perfect opportunity. If they were looking for me, I figured they'd eventually find me. I couldn't have them use me to get to you. And I couldn't have them track me to Marcyville. So I left."

A knot clogged her throat, and her eyes burned. She wouldn't cry though. No matter what, she would hold strong.

Though his face was cast in shadows, she felt his gaze on her. Patient. Waiting. She had to say something. She managed a nod and swallowed enough to speak. "I don't blame you for leaving after you learned the truth."

A long breath seeped out of him, and he turned back to the fire. "Maybe I should've told you. I was just desperate to keep you safe."

She shrugged. "It wouldn't have mattered." Knowing that Ben had learned the truth of her past would have only made her pain worse.

He faced her again, casting his expression in shadows once

more. "I'll not leave you again, Heidi. The others can go back if they want to, though I doubt they will. I'm coming with you. My arm will heal, and I can still help with the sketches. Don't try to run me off or sneak away without me. It won't work."

Before she could answer, the others' voices grew louder, more distinct as they approached the camp.

Maybe it was for the best they were coming back. She had no words to answer Ben. She needed time to process everything he'd said. But she'd not be able to think clearly tonight, not with so much swirling in her mind. She'd rather succumb to the numbness of sleep.

CHAPTER 10

*H*eidi had been right. Her eyes burned as if she'd not slept an hour straight in the night. Her sleep had been plagued with a twisted swirl of dreams and painful thoughts as all her fears and worries resurfaced. She'd thought she left them back in Westminton, but knowing that Ben knew her background—at least in part...

The mist that rose off the water surrounded her where she stood at the river's edge, not thick enough to make her disappear.

The swish of grass sounded behind her, and she turned, her body tensing with the awful possibility that Ben might have come to talk more about what he'd overheard. To ask more questions about her family's sins.

But Temperance walked toward her. T knew nothing about her past. Heidi was safe with her.

She tried to manage a smile for her friend, but the weary muscles of her face wouldn't work as she told them to.

T didn't talk at first, just stood beside her and faced the river. After a moment, she spoke, her brogue thicker than usual this morning. "I'm not sure if t'e way you be tossin' and turnin' all night means t'e others leave us today, or if t'ey intend to stay with us."

Heidi kept her focus ahead. "Ben said he wants to continue the journey. I plan to offer the others a chance to turn back once they all rise this morning." She'd not had the strength to say it last night. She didn't know Lola, White Owl, or Louis very well yet, but she had a feeling they would choose to keep going as well.

If they knew the truth about her past, about the innumerable schemes her family had carried out to steal from good, honest people, they would know she wasn't nearly good enough for them to devote so much of their energy to help. She wasn't up to telling them everything, though. She didn't have the strength to—or maybe the courage. Bad enough Ben knew. No wonder he'd hightailed it out of Marcyville first chance he got. He'd said he wouldn't leave her again, but was it only guilt from leaving her the first time?

She slid a look at Temperance. T deserved the truth. She was trusting Heidi with her life, and she deserved to know in whom she placed her faith.

Heidi stared into the mist, swallowed the lump in her throat, and summoned every bit of bravery she had left. "There's something you should know about me. Something I should have told you before you left my aunt's to come west with us."

She dared another glance at her friend, but the concern in T's eyes made her regret the look. Once more, she had to swallow to clear her throat enough to speak. "My family...isn't good." How much did she have to say?

"Mr. Martin and Mrs. Bertie?"

Heidi shook her head. "My uncle and aunt are completely unlike my parents. I don't know if my mother was always so different from Aunt Bertie, or if my father turned her that way. But my parents are bad people. They'll lie and cheat and swindle any way they can.

71

"They had my sisters and me steal from people when we were young. I only remember a little of it. When I was old enough to realize I was hurting the people I lied to, I refused. One time I went back and told one man that my mother made me lie. After that, they left me out of it for the most part.

"But my twin sisters are two years younger than I am, and they both thought it great fun to see how quickly they could convince a stranger to hand over money for them to eat that day. As they grew older, their schemes became more and more grand, and my parents doted on them.

"As soon as I was old enough to leave, I came to stay with Aunt Bertie and Uncle Martin. I think my parents let me leave because they were afraid I would do something to reveal the depth of their thefts to the authorities. They'd always managed to cover up the evidence enough that they never got caught, or if they did, the accusations didn't stick."

Somehow the telling, speaking all of it aloud, lifted a tiny bit of weight from her chest. But now she had to face Temperance. Bear the depth of her disappointment.

She stiffened her resolve, then turned to her friend.

T's face was solemn, impossible to read. Then she raised her brows. "Is t'at everyt'ing?"

Everything? It was nowhere near everything, but did Temperance really want her to detail every one of their sins?

She shook her head. "There were so many things they did to hurt people, by stealing usually. They're probably still committing those crimes, at least they were when I finally got away. Last night, Ben told me he learned that people in important positions are looking for me, for my parents and sisters. They want—" She couldn't bring herself say they wanted her to hang. "They want retribution. I understand if you'd rather not work with me. If you'd like to go back to Marcyville, or even back to your family in New York City, I can arrange an escort and transportation for you." Though how she'd do that from here, she had no idea.

Yet Temperance deserved the chance.

But her friend's jaw dropped, and her expression shifted to something like incredulity. "T'e only way I'd let you send me back to New York is in a wooden casket, and don't bot'er, there's no place to bury me t'ere."

She straightened, her face taking on that determined look that Temperance wore so well. She even propped a hand at her waist. "Your folks sound like the kind of people I'd rather spit on t'an look in the eye, I'm sorry for saying so. But from everyt'ing I just heard, you didn't take part in any of t'ose doings when you had a choice."

She pointed a finger at Heidi and narrowed her eyes. "But the t'ing I do know to be true is t'at you, Heidi Wallace, are an honest, hard-working, and generous woman. T'e kind of person who's the exact opposite of t'a way you describe your family. It's not your Mum and Da I'm traveling through t'ese Rockies with, it's you. And I'm honored to work at your side."

The tears sprang so quickly, Heidi could barely hold them back. One broke through and slid down her cheek. "Temperance, are you certain? I'll do everything I can to get you a new position if you want to return. I won't blame you for doing so."

Temperance gripped Heidi's hand. "You couldna stop me from staying if you tried."

A smile tugged onto her face, and she sniffed away another trickle of tears as she squeezed T's hand. "That's what Ben said, but I don't think he said it for the same reason."

T's brows shot upward. "I 'spect he didn't. What's t'e tale about t'e two of you? Ye know I've been dyin' to ask."

Heidi released Temperance's hand so she could wrap her arms around herself to fend against the morning's chill. "He was a good friend to me when I moved to Marcyville. We were...close. I once thought we would marry, but..." She shook her head again. "I learned last night why he suddenly turned distant, then came west and be a missionary with his sister. He found out about my parents."

Temperance let out a sound of understanding, but Heidi had to look away. T might see how bad it still hurt.

A moment of silence passed before Temperance spoke again. "He told you t'at's why he left back t'en?"

Heidi shrugged, tightening her grip on her arms. "Pretty much. He said he was trying to protect me, to keep some law men he met from tracking me down. But if that were the case, he could've told me back then.."

"Hmm." Temperance dragged out the sound as though she were thinking. "It seems to me if t'at's the way he still felt, he wouldna be workin' so hard to help you now. He wouldna traipsed along on t'is journey, or at least he'd surely be turnin' back now he's hurt."

Heat crept up Heidi's neck, mostly from the insinuation in Temperance's tone. She shook her head to ward off the idea. "He's a good man, always has been. Ever willing to help someone in need. I should've known he would feel obligated to continue with us. He's stubborn like that."

"Obligation, huh?" Temperance gripped Heidi's forearm, forcing her to turn and face her friend. "Heidi, what would happen if ye and Mr. Ben start fresh? Set aside everyt'ing from t'e past and give t'e man a fair chance wit just exactly t'e way t'ings are today. Do ye think t'at's worth a try?"

Once again, that weight pressed on her chest. She knew exactly what would happen if she let her guard down. She would be smitten after a single conversation. Ben would have the power to break her heart again, and this time she might not survive the blow.

~

*S*omething had changed. But Ben couldn't quite put a finger on what that was.

He eyed the set of Heidi's shoulders as they rode along the riverbank. Their entire band had just set out—later than usual, for Heidi had insisted she speak with the entire group that morning. She still felt it necessary to ask them all to turn back, but thankfully none of the others wanted to. Perhaps White Owl and Lola and Louis hadn't been needed in earnest yet, but their presence would probably be a benefit at some point on the journey.

At least Heidi hadn't pushed as hard to send them away as she had with him last night. He still wasn't certain telling her everything he'd learned had been wise. It had lowered the defensive barrier she usually carried like a shield against him. But though she no longer looked at him with the combination of wariness and anger, there was such a sadness about her, it felt like the distance between them had grown wider.

Yet every now and then, she would look his way with an expression that held something dangerously close to hope.

Or maybe the hope was his own. Could she be softening toward him?

Perhaps now that he'd told her everything, she simply needed time to absorb it all. The news had surely dealt a blow. Maybe she had more questions. He could ask her tonight.

Whatever she needed, he would be here to supply it.

Heidi rode just ahead of him, and as she crested the hill they climbed, her demeanor changed and she reined in her horse.

His body tensed. They'd entered a section more hilly than before, and they'd been watching the distant peaks grow nearer. As he reached Heidi, what had halted her came clear.

The bluff they stood on sloped gently to a level plain. But just beyond rose a rocky cliff that would be impossible for their horses to climb. They'd finally reached the first of the peaks.

He'd never traveled this far north, and these were even more majestic—and treacherous—than the mountains farther south.

"The horses won't be able to climb that." Her tone added a silent *will they?*

White Owl shook his head. "We'll need to cross the river."

Ben shifted his focus to the water. The Marias spread wider here than in other areas they'd passed. He couldn't tell how deep it ran.

"You think the horses will need to swim?" Louis asked.

"Let's hope *you* don't have to swim or I'll be pulling you out again." Temperance sent Louis a look that was almost teasing, her tone bolder than what she used to speak to the rest of them, except for Heidi.

Louis met her gaze and held it, a grin playing at his mouth. Was something brewing between those two? He checked to see if Heidi had seen the look, but she was staring out over the river, apprehension tightening her face.

She couldn't swim.

He dropped his voice a little so she would know he spoke to her. "Even if the water's deep, the horses should be able to carry us with no trouble."

She nodded, her brow still furrowed. "I guess we should hold the drawing books over our heads. Maybe wrap them in more oil skins."

Yes, keeping them dry would be tricky. "Sounds like a good plan."

Louis nudged his horse down the slope but called over his shoulder. "I'll cross first and see how deep it is."

As they all reached the flat land, Louis headed toward the narrowest section of the river. He didn't hesitate at the water's edge, just guided his horse in.

Ben waited beside Heidi on the bank as they watched Louis's progress. The water rose to his gelding's chest, and before he'd reached two-thirds of the way in, the animal began swimming.

He had to force himself to breathe as the pair progressed. Was it only his worry that thickened the air, or did Heidi's fears taint his own? Louis had proved himself an able swimmer, and even now he'd moved out of the saddle and swam with one arm while he gripped his horse with the other. He would make it across fine.

At last, the horse found solid footing on the other side, and Louis swung back into the saddle as the gelding struggled through the shallows. Once the pair stepped up onto the far bank, Louis turned and waved. "Come over. The crossing's easy."

Heidi snorted just loudly enough to reach Ben's ears.

Ben offered his own chuckle. "It's easy, he said." He glanced around at the rest of the group. "I can go next. I'll take one of the packs that shouldn't get wet and hold it above my head." He looked to White Owl. "If you can do the same, we should be able to keep the important things dry."

His gaze caught on little Anna, then moved back to White Owl. "Unless you need to carry your daughter. I can come back for another load."

"Anna and I can manage fine." Lola spoke up. "I'll strap her in the cradle board and hold that above the water like you're doing with the supplies."

"But you can't hold a pack above your head with your arm in the sling." Temperance frowned at him.

Ben sent her a confident look to set her mind at ease. "I'll hold the reins with my left hand and the pack with my right. I can use the left hand even with the arm in a sling."

"I'll carry the pack. You rest that arm." Her tone sounded far more like the way she spoke with Heidi.

He couldn't help but grin. "I can do it. I promise."

Her eyes narrowed. "I'll carry the pack."

Ben let out a breath. "If you insist." She'd proven herself

capable. She should be able to manage if the water cooperated. He could step in and help if necessary.

And he also had to make sure Heidi reached the other side safely.

He met her gaze. "Do you want to cross at the same time I do? When you get into the deeper water, keep a firm grip on your saddle and let your body drift behind you in the current."

She nodded, though she didn't speak. She wouldn't confess her fears unless they were unbearable.

Once they had the packs re-sorted, he glanced at Heidi. "You ready?"

She nodded, still not speaking.

"We'll file in behind you two." Temperance halted her horse behind Heidi's.

"Let's go then." He nudged the big gelding forward, and Heidi reluctantly signaled her mount up with his.

Together, their horses stepped into the water.

CHAPTER 11

*T*he knot in Ben's gut eased as the animals moved smoothly through the water. All their mounts were well-mannered for the most part, and likely tired from so many hours on the trail each day. At least his injured mare had stopped limping, though the gash was healing slowly.

As they reached the deeper water that came to the gelding's chest, Ben glanced back at the others. Lola rode behind him, little Anna in her cradleboard raised high. Beside her, Temperance held up one of the packs they hoped to keep dry. Bringing up the rear, White Owl did the same. His bundle was larger than Temperance's and contained the main book of drawings Heidi had filled with detailed maps. If anything happened to that bundle...

But he turned forward again. Best not to borrow trouble.

Heidi's mount began swimming first, and Ben's did the same a step later.

The big gelding's stroke was as strong as his walking stride, and he pulled a little ahead of Heidi's horse. Ben kept half his focus on giving the gelding the rein he needed to maneuver and the other half on Heidi.

She clutched tightly to her saddle and reins but let her body float with the current as he'd said.

He raised his voice above the water's flow. "You're doing fine."

She gave him a grim look, but there was more determination in the expression than fear, so he eased out a breath.

Behind them, White Owl called to his wife, but Ben couldn't hear the words over the water. From Lola's response, he must have been simply checking on them.

At last, the big gelding's hooves found solid ground, and Ben struggled to get his legs on either side of the saddle as the horse emerged from the water. Having one arm strapped in the sling made it harder to find his balance.

From the corner of his eye, he saw Heidi's horse rising from the water—riderless. He turned to search for her, but she was walking on the horse's other side. She must not have managed to get astride in time.

"Are you all right?"

She still clutched the saddle, and her skirts seemed to slow her down so she half-walked, half-dragged away from the animal. "I'm fine. Just wet." She sounded out of breath.

Once they reached dry ground, he allowed a long breath to seep out as he climbed down from his gelding. Water dripped from all the animals, and Heidi still clutched her horse's saddle as if she couldn't stand alone yet.

"Should we build a fire to dry things out?" Louis looked barely wet, that familiar grin marking his features.

Heidi shook her head. "I'd like to keep moving if we can. I don't mind drying while we ride." She glanced around the group.

Lola answered for them all. "Of course. I'll change Anna's diaper while you readjust the saddle packs."

Moving things around again didn't take long, but Ben spent

an extra minute readying his sketchbook and pencil in the pack so he could easily reach them with his good arm.

A motion on the other side of the gelding grabbed his focus. A quick movement near the shrubs at the top of the ridge that extended along the river's edge.

Nothing moved now, but his body tensed. It could've been only a rabbit or squirrel or bird.

But it might have been a stranger. One of the Blackfoot they'd been warned so much about.

He eyed the area for several seconds, scanning the ridge in both directions. Nothing.

Maybe it really was a harmless animal. This feeling could be an excess of caution left over from the tension of the river crossing, but his gut told him to mention it to White Owl.

He moved to White Owl's mount, where the man was adjusting the pack behind his saddle. White Owl raised his brows at Ben's presence but didn't ask the obvious question.

Ben cast his eyes toward the ridge without moving his head. "I thought I saw a movement up that slope. Maybe an animal or something I imagined. We've been watching for Blackfoot though. Is it better to see if something's on the other side or go on about our business until they make themselves visible?"

White Owl didn't look that direction as far as Ben could tell, just pulled his last strap tight. "I will see what is beyond. Stay with these."

Ben glanced around the group as he moved back to his gelding. He should pretend nothing was happening.

While Louis finished with his pack, Lola, Temperance, and Heidi were cooing to little Anna. As the Shoshone brave crept up the hill, Louis caught sight of him. His brows lowered, and he darted a look to Ben.

Before Ben could motion for him to stay quiet, Lola also noticed her husband's stealthy movements. Within seconds all were watching him. Thankfully, they seemed to realize the need to stay quiet.

When White Owl reached a place where he could carefully raise his head above the ridgeline, he slowed, easing upward a fingertip at a time. He finally stopped moving and held motionless for what felt like a full minute. Maybe longer.

Then finally, he eased back down, creeping just as quietly as before. Did that mean he'd spotted something—or someone? If there was no concern, wouldn't he walk back to them with a normal step?

When he reached their group, they gathered around him. White Owl's gaze met his wife's first, then slid from one to the next. He wasn't like so many men, ignoring the women as though their thoughts or concerns weren't as important as a man's.

At last, he spoke. "There is camp in valley. They have seen us and are gathering."

"How many?" Louis got the question out just before Ben could ask his own. "Do they look friendly?"

White Owl held up both hands, all ten fingers splayed. "This many lodges." He met Ben's gaze. "Blackfoot will ready for war unless we tell them peace."

Ben turned toward his horse. "Let's tell them then. I'll ride out with you." He looked back at White Owl to make sure he was of the same mind. They'd done this once before when approaching a band of Flathead, though that tribe wasn't usually as warlike as the Blackfoot had a reputation of being.

White Owl gave him a single nod.

"I can come with you." Louis stepped forward.

Ben eyed the young man. "It would be better to have a man here." He didn't speak the final *just in case*, but Louis seemed to hear the words, for he nodded.

As White Owl turned to his wife and took her hand, Ben

focused on his horse to give the couple a moment alone. Lola would surely worry for her husband.

Maybe Ben should offer to do this alone, or take Louis with him. Was it really fair to put a man in danger whose wife and infant daughter depended on him, just because that fellow happened to be well-versed in the sign language all these tribes used to communicate?

But before he could raise the question for the Lord's guidance, Heidi moved toward him. The concern in her gaze was evident as she reached him. "What will you do? Ride out to meet them?"

He nodded. "That's usually the way White Owl likes to face a new group. We treat them as friendly unless they prove otherwise."

The concern in her eyes turned to something much stronger. "But what if they attack you? Have you ever met tribes with the reputation of the Blackfoot in this area?"

A recollection brought a smile. "Goes Ahead. His tribe, the Gros Ventre, aren't known for their friendliness, especially toward the Salish tribe we were living with at the time."

The rest of that memory settled, bringing a wash of pain. "We returned to the village from a short journey away and found all of our Salish friends massacred. Goes Ahead was standing there at the edge of the camp with his tiny daughter in his arms. We thought he was one of the killers at first. He was grieving his wife and worried about his two children, and he didn't make it easy for us to get to know him." Those had been hard days, but so much good had come from them.

A tiny smile touched Heidi's mouth. "I guess you eventually realized he was good?"

That last word caught him. Had he ever thought of people as good or bad? A Scripture slipped in. *No one is righteous; no not one.*

How could he explain this to Heidi. "No one is *good,* but God

83

revealed himself to Goes Ahead in a very personal way. It was at that point when I began to trust him, but I confess it took me more time—and more nudging from the Lord—to trust him with my sister."

White Owl mounted his horse, the sign he was ready to go. Ben touched Heidi's arm, an action he wouldn't have attempted yesterday. "Pray for our safety. Hopefully these will turn into new friends."

She looked doubtful. "Be careful." She truly did seem to be softening toward him.

He forced himself to turn away from her and mount his gelding. As he and White Owl rode up the slope, he glanced at Heidi once more. She stood with Lola and the babe on one side and Temperance on the other, Louis just beyond her. A line of friends, praying for their safe return. He offered a friendly salute, then turned to the task at hand.

As they crested the ridge, the village White Owl spoke of came clear. About half the size of Goes Ahead's camp.

A group of riders galloped toward them from the side of the town where a herd of horses grazed. Likely, whichever scout he'd seen at the top of the ridge had raced back to alert the others, then the warriors had run for their horses so they'd be ready for battle if needed.

Lord, let them be willing to meet peaceably.

There were five in the group cantering toward them, but he and White Owl kept their horses to a slow jog as they approached.

He slid a quick look to gauge White Owl's expression. The lines of his features were tight. Strong. Yet White Owl had learned well the ways of diplomacy. He carried a hunting knife in the sheath hanging from his neck, and a tomahawk and rifle dangled from loops in his saddle, but he would use none unless to save his life or that of one of the others in their group.

Ben had a rifle in the scabbard attached to his own saddle

and kept his hunting knife sheathed at his waist. He'd never pointed either at a person, and he could only pray he wouldn't have to this day.

When the natives reached them, they reined their horses to a hard stop. All the men held war clubs, and one of them raised a coup stick high over his head, shaking it toward Ben and White Owl. Ben didn't let his gaze linger on the black scalp locks hanging from the decorated rod.

Instead, he made the sign for peace, as did White Owl. The man holding the coup stick spoke a string of words Ben couldn't understand.

White Owl knew a few words in the Blackfoot tongue, but had he caught any of that rapid fire? He answered with sounds Ben couldn't decipher. They came out slower and more stilted than the other man's, and White Owl accompanied them with signs. One of the motions was *peace* again, and the other gave the word for *water* as White Owl motioned toward the river. He must be telling them they were simply traveling along the river.

We only need peaceful passage. If only Ben could say that in the tongue of these people.

The man who spoke before spouted another stream of words, and his tone didn't sound welcoming, but at least he lowered his coup stick.

White Owl kept his focus on the strangers but spoke English through gritted teeth. "Do we have a gift for them?"

A gift? He and Elise had brought presents when they'd first come west, little trinkets they'd been told the natives would enjoy. But those were long gone. "Like what?"

His mind scrambled through the things in his packs. The sketchbook and pencil lay on top, but those were critical to Heidi's work. She had several spare books, but likely they would need them all for drawings. He had a pack of pemmican and another of smoked buffalo meat—snacks so he wouldn't bother the others if he grew hungry in the saddle. An extra tunic and trousers that had several holes in them. The clothing wouldn't last much longer, but he kept them in case he had an unexpected need. Would they be a suitable gift—or an insult? He also had an extra pair of moccasins, wrapped in a blanket, and the furs he slept on at night. His mind scrambled for anything more.

He might have to give them the sketchbook. He certainly couldn't part with his rifle or hunting knife, not when he would need them on this trek.

Would these men be satisfied with only the pencil? He could show them how it made marks.

An idea slipped in, and he couldn't help but grin as it took root. "I do have something."

CHAPTER 12

*B*en reached slowly for the sketchbook and pencil, careful not to give the warriors any sign he meant to hurt them. Good thing he'd positioned the book on top so he wouldn't have to dig through the pack.

He flipped to a clean page and used the hand of his injured arm to brace the book as he sketched. A decade ago, he'd worked hard to master his ability to draw faces, or at least make them a recognizable likeness.

He now outlined the face of the man who'd done most of the talking. The shape was long and lean, with a strong nose and high cheekbones. He gave the eyes a glint of steeliness to make him look even more like a valiant warrior. Then the pompadour on top of his head flowing into the braids on either side. He wouldn't take time to draw anything below the neck. This would have to do, and though he'd not sketched a face in quite a while, the likeness was close enough. He carefully tore the page from the book and handed it to White Owl.

They'd all been watching him in silence, and as White Owl studied the page, the corners of his mouth tipped upward. "Is good."

A bit of the weight on Ben's chest eased, and he lifted his gaze to examine the next man he would draw. After he outlined the broader, squarish face, he paused to watch the first brave accept the sketch from White Owl.

His brow furrowed as he studied the drawing. Did he even know what he looked like? Perhaps these men had never peered into a mirror or a piece of shiny metal to see their reflection. Would he be insulted by his appearance?

Lord, let him be pleased with the creation You've made in him... and the way I've captured it on paper.

The man looked like he would be studying the page for a while, so Ben returned to his drawing. The eyes on this one didn't come out the way he'd hoped—too beady. He worked on them longer, adding depth and strength. He'd never done portraits for a subject when it mattered, but he'd once heard an artist say, *I simply make them younger and prettier than real life, and I find my services in great demand.*

He could only hope these men prided themselves on their nobility and warrior prowess, for that was the look he was doing his best to imbue with a double portion into these drawings.

When the second man received his likeness, his brows rose as he studied the page. The first fellow looked over his shoulder and spoke something, pointing to the drawing. As the two talked, they seemed intrigued by what Ben had done. Not angry.

He had to move faster with the next three but still give the same level of care to each feature. By the time he finished the fifth, his mind had grown weary and his hand cramped.

But his efforts had more than accomplished his aim. The fifth man accepted his portrait with the same pompousness the others now showed. Each seemed proud of his likeness. They certainly would be the only five in their village to own such treasures.

He glanced at White Owl. "Will they allow us to pass through without harm now?"

White Owl signed to the men and received a quick reply from the one who must be their leader. He smiled and spoke rapidly as he gestured.

White Owl gave a short answer, then nodded. "They will not bother our women and children."

Ben nodded his thanks to the men, and at last, they were permitted to leave. He rode beside White Owl toward the ridge where the others waited. It took everything in Ben to keep from pushing the gelding into a run, just to make sure nothing had happened to the others while he and White Owl were occupied.

At the crest of the hill, he caught sight of Heidi and the rest waiting where they'd left them. In almost the same position.

He met Heidi's gaze, and the relief in her eyes raised a flash of hope within him. If she'd worried about him, perhaps he'd not ruined things completely with her. Maybe—just maybe— she would allow him the chance to start over.

He would never take for granted her affections. But before he could ask for anything more, he had to get her safely through this expedition. And that might well be harder than any of them had thought.

~

"*D*o you think they're watching?" Ben stood next to White Owl, both staring into the darkness beyond the campfire.

The Blackfoot hadn't bothered them as they rode up the river all day, though they'd been close. Ben had seen glimpses of movement, as had the others at various times throughout the afternoon.

He couldn't blame them for wanting to be certain the strangers riding through their territory kept moving and didn't circle back to harm their village. As long as that was all the watchers intended to do—watch.

White Owl nodded. "We should take turns this night."

Set a guard? It made sense, though they hadn't done so on other journeys. This time, though, the danger felt stronger, the stakes higher. Maybe because the Blackfoot in this area had such a reputation for hostility. And if anything happened to Heidi, or any of their group...

Before he could volunteer a shift, Louis joined them. "I can take the first watch. My brother and I used to trade off all the time when we rode together."

White Owl nodded. "I will rise next."

"I'll take the final watch then." He glanced at White Owl. "Wake me if I'm not up."

The corners of White Owl's eyes creased. "I will make sure you do your share."

~

*H*eidi approached Ben as quietly as she could manage in the pale morning light. Maybe she shouldn't disturb him while he stood guard, but with morning practically here, the danger should be over. And she could help him watch as they spoke.

She had to talk with him. Alone.

She couldn't keep going like this, lowering her defenses against his charm, without knowing for sure what he thought about her.

He knew the truth about her past. It had driven him away once. So what had changed since then? Did he really miss her so much?

Or perhaps nothing had altered. Maybe he was just being chivalrous helping her on this expedition. Perhaps this was only kindness—Christian charity toward someone he knew well to be a sinner. Or at least from a family of sinners.

She had to know.

As she neared where he sat on a boulder near the river's edge, Ben turned to her. His eyes looked weary. Perhaps she should have stoked the fire and heated coffee before coming to him. But they wouldn't have long before the others started to rise.

She settled near him, close enough she could reach out and touch him. Not that she would.

Yet as she sat with her legs hanging off the edge of the rock and the river murmuring beside them the memory of their days before hovered near. Ben would start telling her a story about one of his siblings. Or a funny tidbit from his fathers visit to a parishioner. Ben always made her laugh, and she got to know the townspeople through his stories.

Now, though, he waited for her to speak. Should she come right out and ask him? Ask him *what*, though?

What his intentions were? If he'd changed his mind about hating her? If she stated it like that, his chivalrous defenses would rise. He wouldn't admit to hating a woman. "Ben." Her voice rasped from sleep, so she cleared her throat.

"Yes?" He sounded wary. Maybe even worried. What did he think she would say?

She couldn't let his concerns shift her off course. She inhaled a steadying breath. "Why did you come with me on this expedition?" Hopefully he wouldn't give her an easy answer like *because you needed protection* or *because I couldn't stand by and let two women ride off to their death.* Safety might have played into his actions, but there was more.

She hoped there was, anyway.

He rubbed his lips together, staring at the gentle current. After a moment, he turned to her.

She could feel the weight of his gaze on her face, but she couldn't bring herself to meet his eyes.

"I already told you. I left you once, and it's one of my biggest regrets. I won't leave you again."

His words forced her to look at him, though seeing his face made her chest ache with a physical pain. He was so handsome, but more than that, he was *her Ben*. The man she'd loved with every breath, with every part of her being.

The one who'd left her. Broken her heart as if she didn't matter to him. How could he suddenly care now? How could she trust that he really did?

"Would you have ever come back for me? If I'd not come west...? If you'd not stumbled upon us burying Philip...? Would we have ever met again?" She wanted a man who would fight for her. Who would come to find her, no matter how hard the journey. Even if she didn't deserve those things, her heart craved them.

And she wouldn't give in for anything less.

Pain twisted his features. "Heidi, I couldn't put you in danger. I laid a trail west so they would follow me. I took the train back to the closest stop near Westminton and talked to everyone I could, telling them my name and that I was headed to the western territories. Then Elise and I went straight west, stopping in towns along the way, buying supplies we'd need and doing things to make sure people would remember me. Like a breadcrumb trail leading to this land so that if anyone were looking, they'd find me first and hopefully leave you alone."

He swallowed. "I didn't realize how far removed this western territory is from the States. No one has come here searching for either of us that I know of. I think... I think you'd be safe here, especially if we stay away from the places reached easily from the Missouri River. Would you ever... I mean, could you see yourself...?"

Was he asking if she would stay with him? They were

nowhere near that point again. She still didn't know if she could trust him not to change his mind again. Sure he'd refused to turn back from this expedition but...she just needed more time.

He must have seen her thoughts in her expression, for he shook his head. "I know. I don't deserve a second chance. Not after I hurt you." His gaze dropped to the grass ahead of them. "I should've told you the truth. I see that now. But I was afraid if I did... Well, I was afraid you'd be so determined to prove yourself innocent, you'd go back to Westminton. Those men don't care about the truth. They said no amount of money would stop them from making sure you received the worst punishment possible, same as the rest of your family." He looked back at her, his eyes earnest. Pleading. "I just want you to be safe, Heidi. And happy."

A rush of emotion surged to her throat, burning her eyes. A half-laugh, half-sob burst out. "I wasn't happy, Ben. You broke my heart. And wouldn't even tell me why. I didn't know what I'd done. Or if you never loved me at all. If I'd only been deceiving myself. Making a fool of myself."

His eyes glimmered with the pain reflecting there, and he lowered his voice. "Oh, Heidi." He raised his hand and brushed the hair from her cheek behind her ear, sending a shiver through her the way his touch always had. "I'm so sorry."

Those words, more than anything else he could have said, more than even the contact between them... Those words settled over her, soothing the churning in her spirit.

Whether he pulled her closer or she came because of a longing for what they'd once shared, she leaned in, resting her head on his shoulder as he wrapped his arms around her.

Tears slid down her cheeks, but at least she kept in her sobs. "I can't risk my heart again, Ben. Not if you'll push me away when you remember everything you learned about me."

His arms around her stilled, stiffened even. And just as she'd dreaded, he pulled back. Yet not very far. He stopped where he could see her face. The worry marking his brows looked almost painful.

"Heidi, I didn't leave because of anything I learned about you. Or your family. I left because your life was in danger, and that was the only way I could think to save you." He gripped her shoulder and turned her to fully face him. "I need you to hear me on this. There's nothing you or your family did in the past, or could do right now, that would change how I feel about you. How I've always felt. I loved you then, Heidi Wallace. And I still love you now. There's nothing I can learn about you that will change that."

With every word, her throat squeezed tighter. Could he possibly mean it? She could barely see him through her tears, but the rough warmth of his hand cupped her cheek, and she leaned in.

"Heidi, I'm so sorry." He pulled her close again, this time pressing her face to his chest.

Too much emotion welled in her. As much as she tried to hold in the sobs, they slipped through her defenses. Could Ben really love her despite knowing the sins of her family? Had he left her because he wanted to protect her? It seemed too good to be true. Too much goodness to take in.

His cheek rested on top of her head, and he murmured in a gentle voice, though she couldn't decipher the words above the turmoil within her. She had to get herself under control. The others would rise soon—might even be up now.

That thought gave the push she needed to pull back and wipe her eyes. She managed a shaky smile. "I'm sorry to blubber on you."

He reached up and brushed his thumb across her moist cheek. "Can we start over? I don't expect to be able to pick up the way things were between us before I left to take Gretta to school, but maybe you'd let me court you a bit as we travel?"

This seemed too wonderful to believe. She nodded. "I would like that."

He reached for her hand and lifted it to his mouth, kissing the backs of her fingers. "Good."

Though he said nothing more, the warmth in his eyes stirred a longing within her. A longing she'd not allowed for over two years.

CHAPTER 13

"*S*coot over and let me finish that drawing. You're taking too long." Ben gave Heidi's shoulder a playful nudge. Just getting to touch her, even in little ways like this, was something he'd never again take for granted.

Every time she'd looked at him that day, her gaze had been so much softer than before, even shy sometimes. It was those bashful looks that hit him the hardest, warming his insides and making him want to close the distance between them. Would he ever get to kiss her again? He probably still had a lot of trust to rebuild before he earned that privilege.

She lifted her focus from the terrain she was darkening with her pencil on the detailed drawing and blinked weary eyes at him. "Maybe you'd better go on without me. I still have one more section to add."

He gave her a look to show exactly what he thought of that suggestion. "The walk was meant for us to go *together*. Not simply because I'm so eager to see the river."

A smile curved her mouth as she returned her focus to the paper. "I'll work as quickly as I can."

He nudged her again. "This page is large enough, we can

both draw. You sketch the outline of that last area and I'll add in the coloring here to show the terrain."

She scooted over a little, and he dropped to his knees beside her. His shoulder pressed against hers as they worked, a situation he definitely preferred to watching from a distance.

At last, they finished, and he pushed to his feet, then extended a hand to help Heidi up. She bent back over the drawing to darken another area.

He touched her shoulder. "Come on. It's done for the night. You can add more details in the light of day if you want." Dusk was closing in around their campfire.

"Are you two still going for a walk?" Lola sat against a tree trunk, rocking her sleeping daughter from side to side.

"We are." A twinge of pain shot through his left arm as he pulled Heidi to standing. The limb didn't often hurt anymore, but he'd still been using the sling until now. Surely he didn't need the encumbrance for a leisurely walk.

"Enjoy the breeze down by the water." Temperance gave Heidi a raised-brow look that spoke something between the two of them, but he didn't try to decipher it. Just followed Heidi as they left the light of the campfire behind.

During the day's travels, they'd entered a stretch of mountainous country, with stony slopes rising up on both sides of the river. The path they walked now was strewn with rocks and uneven sloping ground. Certainly no wagon road through the prairie like they used to stroll when he'd courted her back in Marcyville.

Over this terrain, he hardly had a chance to walk beside her. Mostly they strode single file, skirting boulders and shrubby trees. Nor did he have a chance to start a real conversation, more than, "Careful" or "Watch that branch."

At last, they stood at the edge of the cliff leading down to the water. The wind here whipped harder since they'd left the protection of the rocky slopes on either side. As he stood next to Heidi in the moonlight, the wide river flowing before them and the wind blowing her hair around her face, calm finally settled over his spirit. The majesty of this land, the untamed beauty, spoke to his soul in a way no landscape ever had. Did Heidi feel the same way?

Before he could find a way to ask her, she spoke. "It's peaceful out here, isn't it." The wind nearly swallowed her voice, belying the words.

"Sort of." In truth, *peaceful* wasn't the way he would describe the overwhelming strength and solitude of this land.

She turned to him, a smile tipping her mouth. "Maybe *invigorating* is a better word." She pressed a hand to her chest. "It eases the unrest inside me. I see why you've stayed."

Was that why he'd stayed? He wasn't finished here, not with telling the natives about God. And he couldn't leave Elise, though she had Goes Ahead now. And Lola and White Owl.

Besides, he couldn't go back to the States, not until he knew there was no danger to Heidi. Of course, he would never know that unless he returned to Westminton to find out.

But the thought of leaving this country pressed a weight inside him. His work wasn't done in this place. Not yet.

"Maybe God was keeping me here until you came. Perhaps He had me stay in that exact village, knowing He'd be bringing you back to me." It was an idea that had slipped in more than once. How, in this vast land that took weeks or months to ride through, had he stumbled upon Heidi, the only woman he'd ever loved, just when she needed him? Only God could have orchestrated that.

She stared over the river as she nodded. "Maybe so." There was a wistfulness in her tone that told him perhaps she and God weren't as close as they'd been before. Had his leaving contributed to that? *Lord, what can I do to help her trust You again too?*

Heidi looked down at the cliff. "Shall we climb down to the water?"

He studied the rock wall beneath them. The surface was uneven, so he might be able to find hand and foot holds to climb down. His moccasins would help his feet grab the stone more securely. But Heidi? Her skirts and store-bought boots would make it hard to keep from slipping.

"I think we'd better not."

But she'd already dropped to her knees and was turning to descend backward.

He gripped her arm. "Wait, I think there's a spot downstream that's not as high."

She stilled and looked where he pointed. *Lord, let that be a safer way down.*

Then she rose to her feet. "All right."

The place he'd seen was a shorter drop to the river's edge, but just as steep. He lowered to his knees. "I'll go first." If he fell, maybe that would convince her not to attempt it.

But the rock face was rough enough that he maneuvered down without having to bear much weight with his injured arm. He jumped the last few feet to the sandy area at the edge of the water. The cliff had been about twice his height, taller than it looked from above.

"I'm coming down." Heidi was already backing over the edge, her boot reaching for a foothold.

He ducked his head to keep from seeing leg amidst her skirts. But if he didn't watch, he wouldn't know if she needed help. So he raised a hand to shield his vision from her skirts, allowing only her boots to show at the edge of his palm.

Her other foot found purchase, and she lowered herself down. One foot, then the next, then the next. She came close enough that he could grip her foot if he needed to, but she was managing. Her boots must not have as smooth a sole as the store-bought shoes he used to wear.

When she was one step away from the ground, he gripped her waist to help her down, as he used to do from his family's wagon. Perhaps he shouldn't have, for the feel of her in his hands made him want to pull her close.

Maybe she felt the same, because when she landed on the ground, she turned in his hands. For a second, they stood face to face, near enough for him to lean in and brush her lips with his. But then she stepped away, turning to the river and moving out of his reach.

She bent down at the edge and ran her fingers through the water. Shadows darted beneath the surface. "Look, fish."

He crouched at her side and peered into the dark liquid. "Too bad I don't have a fishing line with us."

She wiggled her fingers beneath the surface, but the creatures must have all fled. "Remember the time you and those other boys had a contest to see who could catch the largest fish?"

The memory slipped in like it happened last week, and a grin tugged his face. "I still say we should have only counted live fish. Who knows how long that trout Wilson caught had been dead. I heard his mother refused to cook it. Thought it would poison them all."

Heidi's white smile flashed in the darkness. "You put up such a fuss, I was afraid you would come to blows."

He chuckled. "That wouldn't have been a good example from the minister's son. I might have, even still, if you hadn't asked me to let it go."

Her smile slipped, and her voice quieted, some of the mirth leaving it. "I was surprised you listened to me. I think you were the first person ever to do what I asked."

A flash of clarity swept through him. How had he been so blind before? He'd seen her through the eyes of his own life, not looked for the signs of how her past had influenced her thinking.

He let the pretense of humor slip out of his voice. "I'm sorry you never felt heard before, Heidi. I'm even more sorry that I didn't realize it. I was blind and naïve, and didn't see how much you must've been hurting when you first came to Marcyville."

She turned to meet his gaze, her eyes and her voice equally piercing. "But you did see, Ben. You accepted me the way I was, took me as part of your family, and gave me a place where it felt like I belonged."

He reached for her hand, cupping her wet fingers in a loose grip. "You did belong, you still do. I knew it from the beginning and even more so now."

She didn't close her hand around his, just let her fingers lay in his palm as she stared at them. What thoughts clouded her mind? Did she still wonder if she could trust him? Or was she deciding whether she actually *wanted* anything between them again?

Then her hand closed around his solidly, as though she'd made a decision. She met his gaze, her eyes showing that same certainty.

His heart picked up speed, and he rose slowly, pulling her up after him. They stood, face to face. He still gripped her hand, rubbing his thumb across the top of her fingers. She stared into his face, a strength about her—a maturity, maybe—that hadn't been there two years before. She'd always known her mind. It felt as if she'd reached a decision.

She rested her free hand on his chest, and the warmth of her touch singed through his shirt. His heartbeat pulsed hard through his neck, drying his mouth.

Heidi leaned forward a little, leaving no doubt what she intended. But he couldn't make her do the work all on her own. He leaned down, cradling her cheek in his hand, and brushed her lips with his.

∿

*H*eidi had imagined this so many times. Maybe she was dreaming now. But Ben's chest lay firm beneath her hand. Real. The rush of his heartbeat alive under her palm.

His mouth had started out gentle, tentative as it met hers. But now the strength he'd always possessed took over. Drawing her in. Consuming her.

She returned the kiss, losing herself in the heady feeling of Ben. The Ben she'd loved for so long, hers again.

Yet not the same as he'd been before. This Ben held a maturity, a wisdom seasoned by all he'd experienced in this land. She felt in his touch that he treasured her, as if now that he knew what it was to be apart, having her near meant so much more.

Then his kiss eased, softening. He pulled away enough to rest his brow on her forehead as he used to do so often. He brushed his nose against hers. "My Heidi."

The words swirled within her. She *was* his. She'd always been, ever since he'd caught up with her on the way home from school that first day when they were fifteen years old.

He'd opened his life to her, a scared girl desperate to leave the shadows of her family behind. As he gave her his friendship, shared his family and hopes and dreams, she'd responded with her heart. And she'd never managed to regain control of it since.

They stayed like that for a while, and she relished the warmth of his breath, the masculine scent of him, the feel of him beneath her hands—strong and vibrant.

And then he pulled her close, wrapping his arms around her and drawing her to his chest. She rested her head on his shoulder, pressing into the crook of his neck.

This. This was what she'd missed the most. The strength he so willingly shared. The feeling of being so thoroughly accepted. Protected against anything that came after her.

Which was the reason he'd left her behind. Though she still

didn't think he'd chosen the best course of action, Ben had done it for her.

At least they were together again. And if it took staying in this beautiful territory to be with this man she loved, she would do it. Gladly.

Too soon, Ben's breath ruffled her hair as he spoke. "I should get you back before someone comes looking."

She clung a little tighter around him. "I know." But she couldn't make herself release him yet.

After another moment, he brushed a kiss on top of her head, then eased his hands up to her shoulders. She pulled back, missing his closeness already. But with space between them she could stare into his handsome face, shadowed a little in the moonlight. God truly had blessed him with an overabundance of comely features.

He leaned in once more, but this time he pressed a single gentle kiss to her lips. Then another to her brow.

He met her gaze, his eyes shimmering in the moonlight. "With every breath, I thank God He brought you back to me."

She couldn't speak for the clog of emotion in her throat, and maybe Ben realized that, for he released her and turned, sliding her hand in his. She needed to keep this connection as long as possible, and maybe he did too.

He studied the rock face before them, and she did her best to focus on it too. The warmth of his palm against hers was a tempting distraction, but when he pointed to the cliff, she forced herself to pay attention.

"It's like a ladder. One foot here, another there. I think you can hold on to that jut until you climb high enough to reach the top." He glanced at her. "Shall I climb first and make sure it works?"

With his full attention focused on her, her pulse sped again. She couldn't hold in a smile, but at least she managed to sound serious. "All right."

Ben responded with his own grin, and he reached up a finger to brush the tip of her nose. But the touch seemed only to call him in for more, and he leaned for another quick brush of his lips on hers.

She would gladly settle in for a much longer kiss, but he pulled away, squeezing her hand with reluctance on his face. "I'd better get moving."

She released his fingers, then she backed up to watch him climb the rock face. Only when he'd reached the halfway point did she finally pull from the haze of pleasure his kiss created. The tendons at his neck strained as he pulled himself up, one foothold at a time. He seemed to be mostly climbing with his right arm, just using his left to help hold himself against the wall.

His injured arm. How had she forgotten it? Just because he wasn't wearing the sling...

"Are you hurting your arm, Ben? You shouldn't be climbing."

"I'm fine." He'd passed the jut of the rock and now held to the top ledge as he climbed the last steps, then raised his knee onto the flat ground above.

He'd made it. She exhaled a breath. Now she just had to manage the climb too.

Ben disappeared over the top as she placed her foot in the first groove and reached up for the jut of stone. She could just barely reach it but managed to grip her fingers over the top in a hold tight enough to climb the next step, then the next.

"Heidi, wait. I was going to come down and help you up." Ben peered down from above.

She strained to pull herself up as her foot searched for the next hold. "That's silly. You shouldn't be climbing with your arm, and I can do it fine."

"Can you reach my hand yet?" He lay on his belly, right arm stretched down.

She wasn't high enough, so she focused on climbing. One

step, then the next. Most of the footholds weren't far apart, which meant smaller reaches but more of them. She'd nearly arrived at the point where she could place her foot on the jut of rock, then reach up to take Ben's hand and maybe even grasp the ledge.

One more foothold. She placed her right boot on the point of stone and raised her right hand. Her fingers just brushed his, so she stretched farther up to grasp his palm.

Her foot slipped on the rock, thrusting downward. She screamed as her left hand lost its hold.

Ben's bellow echoed in her mind as panic shot through her. Her face slammed into the stone, and time slowed. Her mind registered that she would feel the pain in her cheek later.

But she was still falling.

She grabbed frantically for the rock.

Her leg struck the ground.

Her arm hit next.

Her head slammed and the first shot of pain ricocheted through her.

Blackness closed in.

CHAPTER 14

*B*en couldn't breathe for his panic as he scrambled down the cliffside. He didn't search for hand and footholds, just lowered himself to the jut of rock, then jumped.

Heidi lay crumpled on the ground. She hadn't moved. If she made a sound, he couldn't hear it through the rushing in his ears.

God, no. Don't let her be dead. Not Heidi. If he lost Heidi...

He crouched beside her still body. "Heidi, can you hear me?"

She lay on her side, curled as though she were sleeping.

He brushed the hair from her face. "Heidi, wake up."

She didn't stir, and the heartbeat thundering through him sped faster. What should he do? Shake her? Call for the others? Her head lay on the stone at the base of the cliff. Bile rose up into his throat.

Was there blood? He touched her head, then moved his hand around, feeling through her hair where he could. Not wet. "Heidi, wake up."

Still no movement.

He scanned the length of her. Her arms and legs didn't lie at awkward angles, though her skirts covered much of her legs.

He gripped her shoulder and shook a little, then spoke louder. "Heidi, wake up!"

A groan eased out of her.

A tiny bit of the pressure on his chest eased, and he drew a breath. She was alive.

He shifted her shoulder once more. "Heidi, wake up."

He needed to get her back to camp, but he'd require help to get her up the cliff wall. Even if both his arms had been strong, he wouldn't be able to climb these small handholds with the added weight. They'd need a rope to lift her.

He stood and cupped his hands around his mouth as he yelled up to the ledge above. "White Owl! Louis!"

He paused to listen, his gaze dropping to Heidi. She seemed to be stirring more.

Less than five seconds later, a head appeared above. "What's wrong?"

Temperance. She must have been nearby.

"Heidi fell. I think she's hurt. We need rope and the others to help lift her up."

Temperance mumbled something, but he couldn't make out words as she disappeared.

He dropped to his knees beside Heidi again. He had to get her off the hard rock, and maybe roll her onto her back.

Lifting her head a little, he eased his hand under her hair. Was that a lump behind her ear? While he still cradled her head, he used his other hand to roll her onto her back away from the stone.

Heidi groaned again, the sound deep with pain. Her eyes didn't open.

"I'm sorry, love. I'm trying to be gentle." If she didn't wake, they would need a sling to lift her. They couldn't let her head dangle.

Lord, let her wake up. Let her recover with no ill effects.

He rested her head gently on the softer dirt, then stroked the hair away from her face. Her skin looked so pale in the moonlight. With her eyes shut, she might have been dead.

But she wasn't.

He pressed his palm to her warm cheek to reassure himself. "Wake up, Heidi. I need you to wake up." His voice cracked on those last words. *God, You can't have brought her back into my life only to take her away from me again.*

She didn't move, but the rise and fall of her chest showed her breathing. He straightened her arms, then her legs, studying for any sign of pain that might reveal a broken bone. Hopefully, the blow to the head was the only serious injury, though that was bad enough.

Voices sounded above them, Louis's first, then the rapid staccato of Temperance's panicked brogue. Hopefully White Owl had also come. They would need his strength too.

The moment Louis's face came into view, Ben called out. "We'll need blankets or something to make a sling. She's not awake yet and I think there's a knot on her head."

"We have 'em." Temperance appeared next to Louis. "I'm comin' down."

"No!" He jerked straight. "It's too easy to fall. Drop down the blankets and one end of the rope."

Temperance completely ignored him, turning around and lowering her feet in a balloon of skirts.

Ben's heart climbed back into his throat. "No, Temperance. Stay up there. Please. You'll end up unconscious here beside her. Throw down the blankets, and I'll hoist her up to you."

The hum of Louis's voice sounded above, but Ben couldn't make out the words. Surely he was trying to stop her.

Temperance responded, and the two tones grew heated.

Then she moved back up to safety, turning so her head leaned over the edge. "I'm t'rowing the blankets down first."

Ben caught the first one, then the second as it fluttered into his hands.

"Do you need more?" That voice was Lola's. Maybe it meant White Owl had arrived too.

"Throw down the end of the rope and I'll see. Are there two ropes? If so, throw down one end from each." They had at least two strong cords in the packs. They'd used them both to make shelter from the rain.

One end of a rope sailed down, dangling from above. Then a second.

Now to figure out how to harness Heidi so she'd be safe.

He could lay her on the blanket, then tie each rope to two corners. That would raise her in a sling as comfortable as any he could manage. But would it be secure? If the tie slid off the blanket... Maybe he should cut holes in the cloth to push the rope through.

He spread the first cover on the ground, then the second. Now to lift Heidi onto it.

He moved around to her other side and crouched beside her. "Heidi, love. I'm going to lift you onto the blanket."

She didn't respond, but as he slipped his hands under her neck and legs, another small groan slid from her.

He moved her as gently as he could, adjusting her head, legs, and arms once she lay flat on the covers.

As he stroked her hair away from her cheeks again, her eyes flickered open.

His breath caught, and a surge of relief swept through him. "You're awake." His mouth stumbled over those two words. So much he wanted to say.

You're alive. Please tell me you're not permanently injured. If you leave me again, I might not survive it. Heidi, I love you.

That last part *needed* to be said aloud. He'd not wanted to rush her, but who knew when a moment would be their last together?

He took her hand, gripping it in both of his. "I love you, Heidi. I'll always love you, no matter what happens."

She stared up at him, her eyes unfocused. Her mouth parted like she would speak, but she closed it again. Then once more, she opened her mouth, and this time it was clear she was trying to talk. Was she going to say she loved him too? He could save her the effort, but a selfish part of him wanted to hear those words. Even if they took effort through her pain.

Finally, she made sounds. "W–who...are you?"

The hammering in his heart pounded again. He must have heard her wrong. Perhaps she'd not spoken the words she intended.

He leaned a little closer, stroking his thumb across her fingers. "What did you say?" He needed to get the ropes tied to her blanket so they could take her back to camp and make her comfortable. But since she was awake and talking, he should at least try to decipher her words.

Her neck flexed as she swallowed, then her voice came out a little stronger. "Who are you?"

Pure fear, like shards of broken glass, shot through his chest.

◡

*H*eidi's head pounded, and her eyes felt glued shut as she struggled to open them. When she managed to pry them a tiny bit, the bright light sent knives piercing through her head.

She squeezed her eyelids shut again and groaned.

"'Tis all right, Heidi. You just rest t'ere and wake up when you're ready. I've got your favorites cookin'. Sweet cornbread cooked in pork renderings. I don't have any buttermilk to go wit' it, but t'e tea will help t'at headache you're bound to be fightin'."

The voice. It had a familiar ring to it, but she couldn't place whose it could be. Mama spoke so much rougher. And not with that foreign lilt either. Of course, Mama could shift accents when needed. Were they in public somewhere?

Thinking so hard only made her head pound worse.

Another voice sounded, a woman speaking quietly. "I'll take her now. I think she's hungry." Did she sound familiar too? Maybe. It all ran together. She must be out among other people though. The first woman might be Mama distorting her voice to trick the other lady.

A baby fussed. Whose baby?

She pried her eyes open again, this time squinting so the light didn't hurt as bad. She could see the figure of a woman leaning over...a fire? Not in the hearth. They were outside, so it must be a campfire. All these hills and trees didn't look like Westminton though.

Were they traveling with others? Her parents wouldn't usually camp outside. They'd swindle some poor soul into purchasing train fare for the family. Maybe one of the twins would feign illness and Pa would have a tragic tale about how they had to reach a certain physician or the girl would die in a few days.

Or maybe they'd used *her* this time. Was that why her head ached so? Had they given her some kind of poison powder to put her unconscious so they could convince an unsuspecting victim to give money? That would be a new low even for her family.

The twins often pretended illness, or even insanity as part of a nefarious scheme. But none of them had ever intentionally hurt themselves to fool another person. Heidi certainly wouldn't have let them do that to her, nor would she have contributed to one of her parents' plans in another way.

Her chest tightened. Had they hurt her because she refused to comply? Maybe Mama had slipped the poison into food or drink.

That familiar awful feeling rose into her chest, then up to

her throat. She hated her family. Hated the way they took such delight in hurting people. In stealing, whether the victim could afford to lose the money or not. She had to get away. Had to find a way to free herself from the prison of life like this.

Another voice sounded, a little distant. This one a man's. "Has she awakened?"

Something about the sound grabbed her. She'd heard that voice before. It certainly wasn't Pa's. Someone else from town? His tone sounded kind, which wasn't the way any man from Westminton would speak to her family. The Wallaces were hated everywhere they were known.

"Yes, sir, Mr. Ben. She opened her eyes but closed t'em right back. She's stirrin' though."

She forced her eyes open again, at least a little. The man stepped toward her, then lowered to his knees by her side. She tensed. Would he be angry with her?

"Heidi."

Something touched her fingers. It was him. He picked up her hand and held it.

She jerked away. Did he think he could take advantage of her while she was hurt? She would get away no matter what she had to do, no matter how bad she felt.

But he didn't reach for her again. Instead, he spoke. "Heidi, do you remember what happened?"

What happened? She strained to pull up the last memory.

She'd been hanging, wrapped inside a huge sack, or...maybe wrapped in a blanket that dangled. Had she fallen? She must have. That must be why her head pounded.

She had to find someone she knew. Someone who could tell her what in blazes had happened. Someone who could tell her where she was and why.

"Where are...?" Her voice rasped so much that even she could barely understand it. She cleared her throat. "My parents. Where are they?" That was better.

As she squinted, she could only make out the dark outline of the man. The sun behind cast him in full shadow. Maybe if she could see his face without squinting, she would recognize him.

"Your parents? I have no idea. You don't remember where you are? We're in the Western Territory. Do you recall you came west with Temperance and...your cousin, Philip?"

The Western Territory? Where had her parents brought them to now?

She strained to sit up, despite the pounding in her head. "Where are my parents? My sisters?"

"Heidi, don't. Lie back, you're still recovering. You need to lie still." The man put a hand on her shoulder, and the pressure released an alarm within her.

She scrambled sideways, anything to get away from him. Would he forcibly restrain her?

"T'ere, lass. Don't ye be worryin' any. You're safe here." That was the brogue of the first woman, the voice that sounded so familiar. Soothing.

She moved to take the man's place, and he backed away.

Heidi had to at least sit up and figure out where she was. Lying here with the sun in her eyes, she couldn't make out faces.

She held out a hand to the woman. "Will you please help me sit up?"

She hesitated. "I think you'd be more comfortable lying."

If she wouldn't help, Heidi would do it herself. She pressed her hands to the ground and worked to lift her head and shoulders.

"All right t'en. If it be t'at important to you." A hand gripped her upper arm and pressed against her back, helping her lift upright.

Her head felt as if a blacksmith pounded it against his anvil, but she did her best to ignore the flashes of light and shooting pain.

"T'ere's a tree to the right of ye, if ye want to turn and lean against it. That way ye don't have to hold your head up."

Slowly, she turned her head enough to see the trunk from the corner of her gaze. Even that small movement sent a fresh knife of pain through her skull.

But she managed to shift against the rough wood, with the woman helping her. She placed a blanket between her head and the tree for padding.

At last, Heidi could breathe out a long sigh, releasing some of the pent-up air. Now she could see both the man and the woman, and the other lady sitting against a tree a little behind them. From the tiny legs peeking out under a blanket, she must be nursing the babe Heidi had heard.

She turned to the pair nearest her. "Who are you?"

The two exchanged a look full of...worry? Then the woman turned to her. "I'm Temperance, Miss Heidi. Ye had a bad fall off a cliff and hit your head on a rock. It seems like maybe some of your memory left you." She took in a deep breath. "I guess maybe you'd better start with tellin' us what you do remember. T'en we can go from t'ere to fill in the details."

CHAPTER 15

*H*ad she really lost her memory? Did she know these people and not recognize them? Heidi had heard of such, but was it more likely they were swindlers like her parents and trying to take advantage of her?

She lifted her gaze to the area around them. They'd camped in an area with a few trees, and beyond on either side rose steep mountains covered in craggy rocks.

There certainly weren't mountains like these in Westminton. But she'd heard of them in the western territories.

She turned back to the woman and man. "I don't know what I remember. Just normal life. Are you traveling with my family?"

The man leaned forward. "Do you remember coming to stay with your aunt and uncle?"

She strained to recall. "The only aunt I know of is my mother's sister. She lives in Illinois, I think." Mama never spoke kindly of her. Said she married above her station and thought she was too good for the rest of her family.

That life didn't sound so bad to Heidi. She would love to be a better person than her parents and sisters proved themselves every day.

The man was watching her with a gentle sadness in his expression. "You went to live with them—your Aunt Bertie and Uncle Martin—when you were fifteen. That's when you and I met. We used to study together and became good...friends." His voice paused before that last word, as though he'd almost said something else.

She tried to raise a memory of him. *Maybe* she remembered. His face certainly possessed something that drew her, more than just his handsome appearance. There was an earnestness in his expression, a gentleness. If she didn't know him, she would like to. "What is your name?"

His face fell at her question, and hurt clouded his eyes. "Ben. I'm Ben."

Regret tightened her throat. She'd not meant to bring him pain, her mind just felt so thick, she couldn't wade through to find the details she apparently should know.

Maybe if she asked questions, her memories would return. "How long have we known each other, Ben?"

He looked like he was trying to hide his sadness under a forced smile. "I was fifteen when you came to Marcyville, so seven years. I've been away for the last two, and we just found each other again when you came west."

It couldn't be true—none of it. If what he said was true, she'd lost a whole section of memories. Maybe eight or nine years' worth?

But...had she left her parents? Finally escaped her awful life in Westminton? That had to be good. Surely she'd found a better home in this Marcyville place they spoke of. These seemed like nice people. Her new friends?

She turned to the woman. "You said your name is Temperance? How long have I known you?"

As the red-haired woman with the lilting brogue recounted their friendship for the past two years and how they'd come west with her cousin—a cousin she had no memory of—Heidi did her best not to let panic take over.

Maybe they were speaking lies but...she couldn't find her last memory. Her mind felt muddled like she was wading through a thick foggy mire. Her head ached. She *must* have fallen as they said. A blow hard enough to shake away memories from nearly a decade of her life.

How could she recover these missing years? She didn't even know who she was. Part of her wanted to stand up and fight to win back what she'd lost, but how? She couldn't fight her own mind.

Besides, her head was pounding harder now. Just sitting up took so much energy.

"I t'ink you'd best lie down again, Miss Heidi."

She allowed Temperance to help her turn and lie back on the blanket. As she closed her eyes, the blackness eased the unrest inside her.

Maybe after sleep, she would feel more like herself. Or at least, she might know how to recover what she'd lost.

~

"*I* drew this?"

Ben studied Heidi as she stared at the book of detailed sketches. Her finger traced the curving line of the river, moving over the darker shading of the steep bank.

"You did. I never realized you had a talent for drawing. When we were younger, you liked to watch me sketch people. Then you'd try the same, but you never were happy with the outcome." He couldn't help but smile at the way the faces she drew turned out. She would get so frustrated with herself, and he would tease her until she finally laughed and pushed the sketch away.

"I think your cousin Philip taught you, and I'm amazed at

how fast you caught on. You're the expert now, and I'm still learning from you."

She looked up at him. "Can I try it?" She sounded like a child asking permission.

He glanced toward the river. The others had gone for a swim since the day was hotter than most. "I suppose we could walk to the water, and you can practice one of the smaller sketches we do as we are traveling. It's basically an outline of the landmarks with notes about heights and trees and rock structures and such."

Would it be too hard for her to return to the place where she'd fallen? After lying on her bed pallet that first day, she'd been up and moving around the last two. But they'd not taken her to the river yet.

Maybe seeing that place would help her remember something.

Her look turned hopeful, almost girlishly so. "I'd like to try."

He pushed up to standing, then reached to help her. She still moved gingerly. She'd said the headaches had mostly passed, but she might be just trying to keep him from worrying.

When she gripped his hand and allowed him to help her rise, the warmth of her palm against his felt too good. It took everything in him not to pull her in and wrap his arms around her.

He hadn't told her they'd been close like that. A selfish, unreasonable part of him hated that he might have to explain how much they'd meant to each other. Shouldn't it be such an integral part of her that she would know it, even if she'd lost the memories of their time together?

The part of him that loved *her* ran so deep, it was far more than thoughts that could come and go. Or even emotions. His love for Heidi was woven through his core, a part of who he was.

But maybe that was what she'd lost, or at least felt like she'd lost—who she was as a person.

So he didn't pull her into his arms. Instead he released her hand and turned to guide her along the narrow path to the river. He would be here for her, no matter what she needed. He would help her remember who she was. And if God willed it, her memory of their love would return. Either that, or they would build a new love, fresh and untainted by the way he'd hurt her.

The idea slipped through him like a wave of water. Maybe this was God's intention all along. To clear out the memories of how he'd failed Heidi and allow them to build something fresh and lovely.

Warmth eased through him. *Thank You, Father. For sparing her life. For giving us as second chance. If she never recovers her memories, let her fall in love with me again, for I'll never stop loving her.*

Heidi was quiet while they strolled toward the river. Louis's laughter rang out as they approached, and Temperance's brogue drifted after it. The group had discovered a much safer animal trail down the cliff a little farther upstream, so that's what they'd been using to reach the water.

He didn't plan to take Heidi down that path though. Just walking to view the river would be enough. When they neared the edge of the cliff, Ben held out a hand to slow her. "Be careful here."

She halted several steps back where they could see Louis and Temperance wading through the shallows. White Owl, Lola, and the babe weren't in sight, so Ben took a tentative step forward to peer down the cliff at the bank. There they sat at the water's edge.

When Heidi did the same, he couldn't stop himself from gripping her arm to secure her, just in case the height made her dizzy and she toppled forward.

But she didn't, and when she straightened, she turned a hesitant smile on him. He eased his grip on her arm, and allowed his thumb a single stroke before pulling away. Her expression didn't turn worried or fearful from his touch, as it had that first time she'd awakened in camp.

Good. Maybe he'd gained her trust.

He held out the sketchbook and pencil. "Do you want to sit and draw?"

She nodded, and he helped her settle in the grass.

He plopped beside her and pulled out his own drawing book. Maybe if he attempted the same scene, she could look on and see how he started by sketching the larger landscape pieces, like the lines of the river, then added in detail afterward.

But she didn't need his guidance. Her pencil moved slowly at first, speeding up as the river took shape with her strokes, then the bluff on the other side.

He would much rather watch her draw than focus on his own drawing, and it appeared she wouldn't need encouragement or guidance to recall how to recreate the landscape.

She was adding more detail than they usually included in the outlines they made as they rode, more like what she would add to her elaborate drawings at night.

He leaned in and pointed to the bluff. "What you normally do when you draw while on horseback is to shade a corner of this to show its topography, then draw a line along the length that will be filled in with that same shading."

She studied the page, a frown showing her focus on the area. Then she stroked her pencil across the length of the bluff. "Like this?"

"Exactly." He leaned back as she proceeded to outline the features of the mountain rising on the opposite side of the river. It seemed this part of her past, at least, had been ingrained so deeply in her, it returned by instinct.

If only her memories of him and their love had been such a vital part of her. But did he really want them to return if they brought back the pain he'd caused?

∼

*R*iding with Temperance on her right and Ben on her left made Heidi feel fragile.

Every day still seemed like a dream she couldn't wake herself from, but she'd been able to find snatches of memories. Quick images that flashed through her mind and allowed her to grab hold before they disappeared. Aunt Bertie and Uncle Martin resting in their parlor. Her sitting in a boat with Temperance and Philip as strange men rowed them up a river.

Maybe soon the rest of her memory would return. She had a feeling there was something important she'd lost, but she couldn't quite grasp it. She'd asked Ben—he'd been so kind helping her remember other things. But he'd looked startled, almost wary, when she posed this question. Maybe she could find a quiet moment to ask Temperance.

She'd finally managed to learn they were on an assignment to draw maps of the land along the Marias River. Ben hadn't said it in exact words, but she'd gathered they were in a hurry to finish before the weather turned cold.

This was the first day she'd managed to convince everyone she was well enough to travel again. Even if she felt fragile, she would grow strong soon enough.

Ben pointed to a flat area just before a rocky slope rose up in front of them. "This is the mountain White Owl said was too steep to attempt. They crossed the river here."

The land on the other side of the Marias looked level enough for them to maneuver past this obstacle. White Owl, Lola, their daughter, and Louis had already disappeared into a cluster of trees.

As they rode forward, Louis appeared on the far bank, riding back toward them at a canter. His horse splashed through the water, slowing as it reached the deeper current. They met him as he rode up onto the bank.

"We can't pass on that side of the river." He heaved to catch his breath. "We met a band of Blackfoot warriors who said we're not welcome."

Heidi looked to Ben, his expression a blend of determination and apprehension. Blackfoot warriors. Were they dangerous?

"Are the others coming back too?" He scanned the far side. "There they are. What does White Owl say we should do?"

Louis motioned toward the mountain near them. "We'll have to ride away from the river and find a way around that."

As they waited for White Owl and Lola to cross the water, she studied the mountain. It's slope was too steep for the horses to climb, and it looked like at least half a day's ride around. Maybe longer. She could only see one side.

When White Owl and Lola reached them, he motioned for them to follow as he rode away from the river and started skirting the base of the mountain. Their horses picked carefully over rocky ground scattered with shrubby evergreens.

When they'd traveled a quarter hour, she glanced back at Ben. "Should we stop and sketch a map of this area?" They'd done so twice as they'd traveled that morning.

His brows drew together. "In the past, you've only drawn the land right beside the river on both sides. I hope once we reach the Marias again, we'll be able to see its path behind us and can draw what we missed."

The sun shone directly above them as the tree-covered terrain opened to a rocky downhill slope into a canyon. White Owl didn't pause but guided his mount down the steep decline. Their horses descended slowly as they navigated around boulders and into a shallow stream bed.

The sound of voices drifted in the distance, and White Owl jerked up his hand for them to halt.

She strained to hear, but the high-low sounds didn't make words she could decipher. White Owl's expression took on a hard edge as he motioned for them to turn left, away from the strangers.

He led them down the stream bed.

Every time the horse's hooves clicked on the stone beneath them, she flinched. Could whoever had been speaking hear them? Were these the same group White Owl had met on the other side of the river?

A cluster of boulders stood like a wall perpendicular to the cliff beside them, and he turned them that direction. As they clustered behind the protected section, White Owl slid from his horse. "I go to learn who is here."

"Should I come too?" Ben's quiet voice sounded beside her.

White Owl shook his head. "One can hide better." He turned to his wife, and the two exchanged whispered words.

Heidi looked away to give them a private moment. Her gaze met Temperance's wide eyes. She tried to reassure her friend with a smile, though she had no idea if they would be safe.

White Owl seemed competent though. Surely he would know what to do.

CHAPTER 16

*H*eidi watched with the others as White Owl crept away. Once he moved out of sight, they all dismounted, and Ben stepped to the edge of the rock to watch the man's progress. She started toward Temperance to stand with her friend, but Louis already stood beside her, the two exchanging a whispered conversation.

So, she turned to Lola. Anna slept in her cradleboard, leaning against the rock where Lola sat. The woman looked weary, her shoulders slumped and her hands braced on her legs. Heidi settled beside her.

Some of the fatigue seemed to slip away from Lola as she smiled. "How are you feeling?"

She probably meant how was she faring on this first day out. "Well." She still had the slight pounding in her head that hadn't left since she'd first awakened after the fall, but today's long hours in the saddle hadn't increased the pain.

It was the mental unrest that she struggled with the most. The constant struggle to remember. The endless wondering whether she'd forgotten an important detail. She had to constantly ask questions. At least these friends were kind enough not to show impatience. "Do you think those are from the Blackfoot braves you met on the other side of the river?"

Lola shrugged. "Maybe. Could be someone else. White Owl will find out." Her voice sounded so confident. No apprehension clogging her tone.

"Are you...worried about him? His safety?" What was it like to be married to an Indian?

The lines at Lola's eyes tightened. "I try not to think of it. White Owl is skilled enough to sneak in and out without being noticed. I know he wants to return to Anna and me safely. I have to trust that God is protecting him on all sides." She gave a rueful smile. "I'm certainly praying every second for his safe return."

"Can I ask what it's like living out here? Being married to someone with such a different background than your own?" She hoped her questions wouldn't offend.

But a sweet smile spread over her face as she leaned back against the stone. "I love it. Every part." She glanced at Heidi. "I didn't plan to stay out here when I came west. I was looking for my brother, Caleb. Our father had left him something in his will, and my inheritance depended on me finding him. I planned to locate Caleb, get him to sign the papers, then hurry back and resume my life in Pittsburg."

A light entered her eyes. "But I met White Owl along the way. He was injured and nearly dead. After I helped nurse him back to life, he traveled with us as a guide." She stared at the place where he'd disappeared. "The more I got to know him, the more I fell in love. With him and this land both." She spread her hands. "I haven't wanted to return east since."

What a story. A fairy tale almost. Was it really possible to find a happily-ever-after in real life? She'd never witnessed such a happiness. At least, not that she could remember.

As if Lola had heard her thoughts, she turned a serious gaze to Heidi. "I don't mean to say it's always been easy. Life in this land is harder than back where I had so many more luxuries. But you learn to appreciate the little things. And White Owl is such a strong man of God, with a heart to know Him more and more. He inspires me to seek the Lord, and there I find my joy and strength, even in the hardships."

Her gaze turned earnest, almost pleading. "I know I'm where my Heavenly Father wants me, in these beautiful mountains with the husband and daughter he's blessed me with. I think that's the secret. Seeking the Lord's will until you find the place He has for you. That's where you'll find joy, no matter what comes."

The words sank through her with a peace—a sense of hope—she'd not felt since waking from her fall. Could she find the same certainty? Did God have such a plan for her own life?

Could He plan for her to stay in this land? She'd not considered that, at least not that she remembered. Was this His will for her? Ben had said she'd come west with her cousin and Temperance for the mapping assignment, then she'd be traveling east again to her aunt and uncle's town. But what if she didn't *want* to return?

Her gaze drifted to where he stood, watching for White Owl around the edge of the rock. He was such a good man. Kind and giving of himself when any need arose around him. Why had nothing romantic grown between them? That seemed like the kind of thing she would recall, or at least have a feeling about. Surely she'd seen his remarkable qualities before her fall. And he was so handsome. That alone should have drawn her eye. Had she tried for something more between them, but he'd refused?

He straightened, his gaze sharpening as he peered around the rock. "He's coming back."

She and Lola stood, her insides tightening as they waited.

White Owl finally appeared, concern marking his features as he met his wife's gaze. "We must go. Now."

Ben stepped forward. "What is it?"

126

"Blackfoot warriors. Not who we met before. Maybe from same village. We should not be seen."

Within a minute, they'd mounted, and White Owl led them from the shelter of the boulders, down the tiny creek.

A cliff wall rose on their right, and White Owl studied it as they rode. He must be looking for a place the horses could climb up so they could find better shelter in the trees above.

How much longer would they have to ride away from the Marias River? They had to get back to sketch the area they'd had to skirt around. What would happen if they missed mapping that entire section? Would the company who'd hired Philip be angry? Would they refuse to make final payment? Temperance had said Heidi planned to use the money for living expenses while she established her own mapmaking business.

As they rode, the canyon widened, giving more room for the horses to maneuver. The cliff beside them grew smaller and less steep. At last, White Owl turned and guided them up the slope. Heidi leaned forward in her saddle to allow her horse freedom to maneuver up the incline.

When they'd almost reached the top, White Owl pulled up suddenly, scanning the area around them. After a moment, he led them to ground more level, dotted with trees and boulders.

He pointed ahead. "Go straight from here. I ride back to see if we are past the Blackfoot." He turned in his saddle and shifted his gaze from Ben to his wife. "If you find danger, take cover and wait. I will find you."

As he turned his horse toward the river and wove through the trees, tension knotted in Heidi's middle. Surely his experience in this land would keep him from riding straight into danger. He'd proven himself as savvy and capable as his wife said.

Lola, brave as her husband motioned their group forward, taking the lead. The set of her shoulders didn't show worry, only steady confidence. If only Heidi could find that same courage.

The cottonwoods and chokecherries offered little protection. Strain hung heavy in the air as they listened for any sign of White Owl's return. Or a possible threat.

At least a half hour passed before Ben jerked his attention to the side. "Someone's coming."

White Owl appeared around a cluster of trees, his horse moving at a steady trot. His expression seemed less worried than before.

They reined in to meet him, and he pulled up. "They are gone. We can turn back to the river. I have found a place to camp."

Relief washed through her. At last, they could return to their work. Maybe she and Ben could even ride downriver to sketch some of the terrain they'd passed.

If they could just avoid the Blackfoot, all would be well.

～

*B*en woke to blackness. The night had grown colder than usual, and the single quilt he'd unpacked for warmth didn't fully cover his feet.

Steady breathing sounded from the others, and their campfire had faded to only a few glowing embers. It must be several hours after midnight.

He eased the blanket off and stood as soundlessly as he could manage. They'd camped in a small clearing near the river's edge, but trees blocked their view of the water.

He crept down the animal path. At the bank, he stilled, letting the breeze ruffle his hair with its chilly fingers. A fog had settled over the water, circling him. It seemed like he was the only person for miles.

He inhaled a deep cleansing breath, then blew out, letting the turmoil inside fade away. *Lord, clear my mind and heart. Help me focus on You.*

He inhaled another breath, and a realization slipped in with it. The air smelled of...smoke.

He sniffed again. Definitely wood smoke. He'd not smelled it back at the camp. Maybe clearing his nose with the fresh air and fog here had made the scent stronger to him. Or maybe one of his companions had stoked their campfire.

He turned back and stepped into the trees, sniffing again to see if the smell grew stronger.

It faded.

Could there be another group staying nearby? Just to make sure the smoke wasn't from one of his companions stirring the fire in their own camp, he walked the short distance back to their clearing. The others still slept, exactly as he'd left them. The embers from their fire no longer glowed. No smoke rose from the charred remains.

He retraced his steps to the river's edge and sniffed again. The smell was even stronger now. The wind blew the direction the water's current flowed, so the fire must be upstream.

He started that way, keeping his steps quiet in the grass. The fog and darkness allowed him to see only a half dozen strides ahead, but it also concealed him from anyone else. He strained to hear, but nothing sounded except the rustle of leaves and a distant wolf howl.

Would someone camp right on this path at the edge of the river? Likely, they would take cover in the trees where a fire would be harder to see.

He turned and moved away from the water, stepping carefully between the trees. His heart pounded as the scent of smoke grew heavier.

At last, the flicker of a fire appeared between the trunks ahead. He stepped behind a tree. He was still too far away to see more than a red glow.

Moving from trunk to trunk, he crept closer until he could make out the form of a person covered by a buffalo hide blanket. The black hair crowning the head at one end proclaimed him a native. The person slept, so Ben eased to the next tree. Another figure lay near the first. The face was illuminated by the firelight enough to tell it was a man. A warrior, with lines of black paint marking his cheeks and brow.

Ben eased back the way he'd come, taking care not to make a sound. Leaves rustled beneath his feet, but he'd already retreated enough he could no longer see the fire. Maybe they hadn't heard him.

As soon as he left the tree cover, he hurried along the bank to the place he'd been standing when he first caught the scent of smoke. Should he wake White Owl? Maybe they could get far enough from this new group while they slept that there wouldn't be a chance of meeting them in daylight hours.

But was it so important to avoid every native along the way? Maybe these men would prove friendly, like those from the village who'd been so enamored with his drawings. But with the reputation of the Blackfoot in this area, could he really risk their lives for a possibility?

He strode back to camp. As he moved to White Owl's side, the man sat up. Ben crouched before him and whispered, "There's an Indian camp a little upriver from us. The people I saw were sleeping. Should we wait until morning, or move on while it's still dark so we can avoid them?"

White Owl sat quietly for a moment. "Will be light soon. We cross river before sun wakes."

Beside him, Lola rose and pushed her blanket aside. "I'll get our things packed."

Within a quarter hour—far faster than he would have expected—they'd all risen, packed camp, saddled the horses, and were leading the animals to the river's edge.

He handed Louis his reins so he could help Heidi mount.

She'd mostly recovered from her fall except for her memory, but she sometimes moved slower than usual. Not the determined Heidi he'd always known. He couldn't tell if the hesitation came from uncertainty because of all she couldn't remember or lingering pain from her fall. Either way, she raised all his protective instincts.

If only he could help her regain the rest of her memories. He'd done all he could though, and she seemed to have gathered only bits and pieces of her last few years. She'd not said anything at all about remembering him or their times together.

And he couldn't bring himself to remind her.

If she really loved him—if the Lord had created them for each other, as he'd begun to believe—her affections would grow again. He just needed to give her time.

He gripped her gelding's reins and reached down so she could place her boot in his hand like a mounting block. She touched his shoulder as she stepped into his grip.

He couldn't help but look up as the warmth of her fingers brought his skin to life. She hadn't initiated a touch between them since her fall.

She met his look with a slight smile, then moved her hand to the saddle as she grabbed hold and swung up. He held the horse while she gathered her reins. When she nodded that she was ready, she sent him one more smile, her eyes locking with his in a way that seemed significant. Maybe even flirtatious?

Temperance spoke then, and Heidi's attention turned away.

Had he imagined the meaning in the look?

Regardless, his heart picked up speed as he moved back to his gelding and took the reins from Louis. Perhaps he was already making headway in gaining Heidi's affections.

White Owl led the way into the river, and Ben took up the position he'd ridden the day before—at Heidi's side.

The water glistened in the dim light, and the horses waded

through the shallows. Near the middle, the level rose to his knees, but none of the animals had to swim.

At last, they reached the far side, and White Owl turned north again. The land stretched in a long valley with a grass-covered slope rising in the distance.

Maybe they'd finally be able to resume sketching today without having to dodge bands of warriors around every turn. *Please, Lord.*

CHAPTER 17

*H*eidi studied the distant hills and the way the river snaked through them, then did her best to capture the scene with her pencil. This finally felt natural. Work she could lose herself in.

A horse stomped the ground beside her, tugging at her focus. The others waited patiently on their mounts. She sent an apologetic look around the group. "I'm sorry to take so long." Had she been able to draw faster before?

From atop his gelding, Ben cleared his throat. "Don't rush. You're doing fine. If you feel comfortable drawing on your own, I can move ahead and sketch the next section like I did before."

A flash of memory slipped in. Ben's horse cantering toward them, riderless and with the reins flapping. She strained for more. Something about...

She squinted at him. "Did you fall off your horse when you were drawing? Maybe get bitten by a snake?"

Excitement brightened his eyes. "I was *almost* bitten. This boy shied away in time, but threw me in the process. Do you remember it?"

Relief eased through her. "I think so."

White Owl jerked upright, and she glanced at him. He stared back the way they'd come. "Riders coming," he said quietly.

She craned to see the land behind. In the distance, four specs cantered toward them.

"They're close enough to have spotted us." Tension laced Ben's voice. "Should we wait or try to find cover?"

"Wait and talk. Cannot hide." White Owl turned his horse to face those approaching as he spoke something low to his wife.

"Should we ride forward to meet them like we did with the others?" Ben nudged his gelding.

White Owl walked his animal a dozen steps forward, and Ben reined to his side.

Heidi waited between Lola and Temperance, with Louis on Temperance's other side. She had a rifle hanging from the saddle. Should she draw it? None of the others readied theirs.

The riders reached White Owl and Ben, reining in sharply. All four men wore paint marking their faces in different patterns. Their eyes flashed hostility as one spoke to White Owl in harsh tones. She couldn't make out any words, but their anger didn't require translation.

White Owl responded with a series of gestures and sounds.

Heidi gripped her reins, ready to turn her horse at the slightest sign of aggression from the strangers.

A shout sounded in the distance from her left. At the same moment, the brave speaking to White Owl cried out. An arrow struck his arm.

She spun to find its source.

Across the river, five natives on horseback. Another shout pierced the air, this one like a war cry. The riders charged into the water.

The warriors with Ben and White Owl were already wheeling their mounts, circling around the two of them.

Panic slammed through her, and the frantic look Ben sent her way made her plunge her heels into her horse's sides toward the Indians. She had to help him.

But he shook his head, his eyes frantic. "Run! Toward the mountains. Now!"

She pulled on her reins, glancing back at the others. Should she run away and not try to help Ben and White Owl?

Lola was already turning her horse toward the peaks behind them. "Come on!" She had a daughter to protect. And what could she do against so many weapon-wielding men? Heidi wouldn't be able to do much more though.

"Heidi!" Louis motioned frantically for her to get moving. Temperance had already urged her horse into a run, racing with Lola.

Heidi reined her mount around to follow them, but sent one more glance back as she kicked the gelding.

The four braves had surrounded Ben and White Owl so she couldn't see their faces. Would the Indians keep them hostage? If a fight ensued, maybe Ben and White Owl could escape during the ruckus. The lead warrior still had the arrow sticking out of his arm, crimson running from the spot.

She turned her focus forward again as she reached Louis, and he pushed his horse into a run alongside hers.

The attacking Indians had nearly reached this side of the river, and she had to fight the urge to turn and watch whatever was about to happen.

God, keep them safe. Protect these two good men. An image slipped in her mind of both men lying lifeless on the ground, multiple arrows protruding from their bodies. A fresh bout of panic flared through her, and tears burned her eyes.

No, God. You can't take Ben from me. White Owl either.

Ben... The tears flooded her eyes so much she couldn't see the ground in front of her running horse. She swiped them with her sleeve just in time to pull up where Lola and Temperance had stopped to wait, partway up the slope.

She craned to look back at the scene below.

Shouts and high-pitched war cries echoed over the open land. Men fought each other from horseback, wielding clubs in hand-to-hand combat.

She couldn't find Ben or White Owl. Their horses wandered among the chaos—but no riders. Her heart thundered in her throat so hard she couldn't breathe. Were they dead on the ground?

She had to do something. Why had she run? Ben needed her. He'd been there when she lost her memory, always at her side. But the moment he needed help, she'd fled.

She gripped her rifle and yanked it from the scabbard. "I'm going back." It might be too late, but she had to try.

"No!" Temperance grabbed her arm. "T'ere's nothing ye can do against so many."

"I have an idea." Louis pulled out his own rifle and aimed toward the river.

The gun's report boomed around them, and the melee below slowed as the men searched for the source. Louis worked quickly to reload his rifle, and she strained for any sight of Ben or White Owl.

There.

Far below, Ben was hunched over, running toward the water. But where was White Owl?

One of the braves spotted Ben and slammed his heels into his horse's sides. The animal bolted forward, the man leaning low over its neck. Did he have a weapon in his hand?

God, no! She couldn't watch Ben be stabbed through. But she couldn't turn away.

She had to help him.

With her first kick, her gelding charged down the hill like

he'd been waiting for the cue. As they soared over the open ground, she screamed, a guttural cry not too different from that of the warriors.

She never took her eyes off Ben and the rider closing in. Instead of plunging a weapon through him, the brave scooped him up, throwing him over the front of the saddle as his horse slowed and loped in a wide circle.

New panic closed off her yell as the warrior regained control of his mount and turned back the way the first group of riders had come. Ben was struggling, but somehow the man kept him down across the animal.

The rest of the men still fought, some on horseback and others wrestling on the ground. She had to catch up with the man who'd taken Ben, but she couldn't ride through that chaos.

She pushed her gelding harder, turning him in an arc around the group.

Where was White Owl? His horse had moved far away from the fighting, and his familiar form wasn't among any of the struggling men. He might be one of those fallen bodies lying around, but she couldn't tell for sure at this speed. If so, there was nothing she could do for him now.

But she *could* save Ben.

God, if You care about him as much as he does You, help me save him.

The battle raged as her horse raced past. In the distance, she could barely see the brave, still carrying Ben and traveling parallel to the river.

She dug in her heels, urging her horse faster, though he was probably giving all he had. The sun shone hot. How had the heat of the day come already?

A cluster of structures appeared on the horizon. Not trees. Maybe a village of teepees? The brave must be taking Ben back to his people. What would they do to him?

Could she catch up before he reached the camp? She might be within bullet range now, but she couldn't shoot straight on a running horse.

He was too close to the village now. She would never catch him. Maybe she should pull up and try to get back to the others so they could strategize how to free Ben. But what if his captor planned to kill him immediately? Maybe someone in the village would demand his death. She should find a place outside camp where she could hide and watch.

But a sound behind made her glance back. Two braves galloped toward, not far away.

She was trapped. Panic flooded her mind. What should she do? She and Ben would die together in this village. It wasn't the way she'd planned their life to go, but at least they'd be together.

That thought solidified in her mind, clearing out all others.

She'd *planned* for them to have a life together? Back before she lost her memory?

Yes. They *had* been in love. She could feel it deep in her core.

She'd loved Ben. More than she wanted her next breath. And that love still dwelled within her.

With the realization strengthening her determination, she aimed her horse toward the village. If they were to die in this attack, she needed to tell Ben she remembered how much he meant to her.

∽

Should he fight back, or go along peacefully, like Jesus had with His captors?

Ben was being led through the village, a brave on each side gripping his arms, with several more ahead and behind. Women stood back, giving him clearance, hiding their children behind them. As if he were a murderer who might break free and tear into anyone he could reach.

Lord, how can I show them I don't want to hurt them? I only want to be free. To find Heidi and the others and ride away.

They shoved him toward one of the smaller lodges, then pushed him inside. He struggled to keep his footing, but one of the men grabbed his arm and half-dragged him to one side of the fire ring in the middle.

The man who'd captured him yelled commands. They sat him upright. Another brave stepped inside with a bundle of leather twine in his hands.

The one in charge grabbed it and began wrapping the rope around Ben, trussing his arms against his sides. Around and around, he and another man worked. The cord pulled tighter and tighter, cutting into his skin.

Outside, voices argued in their native language. In addition to the pair tying him, two more men stood behind him, though he couldn't see what they were doing. Probably waiting for him to attempt escape so they could pierce him with their knives.

He would have to bide his time. Maybe he could win them over and be set free. Or he would find a chance for escape.

Lord, give me strength.

The voices outside grew louder. Not just the two arguing, but now many tones rising in volume. Had the other warriors returned?

What happened to White Owl? During the battle, White Owl had made a run for the river and disappeared into the water. Ben had been attempting the same when he'd been swooped up into the air and landed face down, hanging over a horse's neck. Had White Owl made it out of the battle and back to their group?

Or had he been captured and was now being brought into this village?

A small, selfish part of him hoped that was true. White Owl would know how they could both escape. God had given him an innate wisdom that would come in handy right about now.

Figures came closer outside. The first man to duck into the lodge was the brave who'd spoken so fiercely to White Owl when the group first approached them, before the attack.

Even now, his face wore a fierce scowl. He dragged in his prisoner, and Ben's mind struggled to catch up with what his eyes took in. Not White Owl.

Heidi.

No!

They dragged her in as they'd done with him, moving her to the opposite side of the coals in the middle. She looked around frantically until her eyes met his. Her relief was visible in the calming of her gaze, the lowering of her shoulders. It was visible in the way she stopped fighting her captors and let them sit her upright.

The same man who'd brought the cord before arrived with more. Her captors began wrapping the rope around her upper body, securing her like a plucked chicken dangling over a hearth fire.

Helplessness rose up in him. Strangling.

These men might do anything to Heidi. Assault her. Murder her. And he wouldn't be able to stop them.

What time I am afraid, I will put my trust in Thee.

Whatever fear he'd felt for himself had fled. Now, he was only terrified for Heidi. He struggled to recall the Lord's promises for protection.

Have mercy on me, my God, have mercy on me, for in You I take refuge. I will take refuge in the shadow of Your wings until the disaster has passed.

Yes. *Have mercy on us both.*

I cry out to God Most High, to God, Who vindicates me. He sends from heaven and saves me, rebuking those who hotly pursue me—God sends forth His love and His faithfulness.

Heidi was looking his way again, and he met her gaze.

Willed her to see his calm. *The Lord will protect you. He'll get you away from here.*

He couldn't tell if she understood, but maybe they'd be able to talk later, once the commotion settled.

Men still moved around them, and voices murmured outside. Would they bring White Owl next?

But he didn't come. One by one, the braves in their lodge moved outside. All except one, who settled on a pile of furs near the door. He crossed his arms and eyed Ben first, then Heidi.

He must be the guard. Would he allow them to speak? Should Ben start by talking to him, trying to convince him they meant no harm?

That might be best.

Ben cleared his throat and shifted, drawing the guard's gaze.

The man frowned at him.

He chose his words carefully. "We come in peace." If only he could sign the word so the man would understand, but his hands were strapped to his sides. "Peace. I am called Ben." He dipped his chin to his chest.

Heidi spoke up. "And I am Heidi. We aren't here to hurt anyone. We just want to leave in peace."

He sent her a look to quiet down, but she didn't meet his gaze. If their speaking made the man angry, he wanted the attention directed toward him. The less notice these people took of Heidi, the better.

Their guard unfolded his arms and drew a knife from the sheaf hanging at his neck in a single practiced motion. He raised it high and bit out a string of sharp commands, aiming them toward Ben.

Ben dipped his head to show he understood the rebuke. The man wanted silence. They could give him that. For a while at least.

As quiet settled over the lodge, his mind worked through possible ways to escape.

Did White Owl still live? If he wasn't injured, he would find a way to come for them.

What of Louis? The man was still so young. He would want to help, but would he possess the intuition and understanding of these people to pull off an escape?

Lord, don't let him do anything foolish.

CHAPTER 18

*H*ours must have passed by now. Each minute ticked by like a turtle as Heidi baked in the hot, stuffy lodge. The guard had lowered the door flap when curious boys crept close to peer inside.

The space was growing dimmer. Did that mean they'd finally reached evening? Thankfully, she didn't require a chamber pot yet. But when she did, would she be offered one if she asked? Or another way to obtain privacy?

And food. Her middle ached, but at least it hadn't started growling yet.

She'd searched through every possible escape in her mind, but nothing sounded likely. If they could create a distraction outside that would draw their guard, she and Ben could run. They were tied tight from the waist up, but not their legs. And they weren't strapped to any object, just their hands bound to their sides. But what kind of distraction could the two of them manage?

Would Temperance or the others attempt to rescue them?

The thought tied a knot of worry in her middle. Her feisty, determined friend might well undertake such feat. But these

Blackfoot—if that was their tribe—would far outnumber and overpower their small group.

Surely Temperance wouldn't be foolish.

Footsteps sounded near the lodge door, and the flap pulled to the side. A young man entered, maybe around sixteen years old. He carried two bark plates with strips of dried meat on them. After setting one down in front of Ben, he placed the other before Heidi, then turned and spoke to their guard.

They must be changing shifts, for the first man rose and left the lodge without a word to them. The younger brave sat on the fur stack and settled back. When he looked at them, he frowned, then motioned toward the food as he said something in his tongue.

"He wants us to eat." Ben spoke quietly, then leaned forward and used his teeth to pick up a piece of meat.

She eyed her own food, and the pinch in her belly grew stronger. As she leaned forward, the rope around her pulled tighter and she had to suck in a breath to reach all the way down. Her nose brushed the dirt, but she caught one of the pieces in her teeth.

She sat up and had to work the meat around her mouth until she could find an end to bite. Once she gnawed off a chunk, the other part fell to her lap. That piece would be hard to reach with her teeth. Maybe she should have tried to keep the entire portion in her mouth, but she might have never managed to chew.

At least she had plenty of time to work on the meal. The guard seemed to enjoy watching her perform acrobatics and chomp bites so large she couldn't close her lips.

Ben finished before she did and offered a few encouraging words as she struggled through the meal. At least this guard was allowing them to speak a little. Maybe she could find a chance to tell Ben about her realization.

Finally, she finished, and quiet settled in the lodge again. She should speak. Now was her chance. It took everything in her to work up the courage, and she kept her voice soft so she wouldn't raise the guard's concern. "Ben, I remembered something important."

He glanced sideways at her, brows rising a little, though not much. Maybe tempering his responses, also trying not to call their captor's attention.

"I love you, don't I?" The moment the words slipped out, she wanted to bite them back. "I mean... That wasn't what I mean at all."

But Ben seemed to be trying to hold in a grin—and not quite succeeding. "You remembered." He breathed out the words like a sigh of relief. As though he'd been waiting for this moment since she woke from the fall.

A bit of the mortification from her blundering words eased. Had she really been right? But she needed more confirmation before she could hazard saying anything more. If only she could piece together more memories of her time with him.

Or *all* the memories. Would she ever recover everything?

He seemed to realize she was waiting. He sobered his expression. "I didn't want to say anything, not when you clearly had no memories of us. I thought if some part of you deep inside wanted to forget..." Pain pinched his features and he swallowed. His chest lifted with a deep breath. "I prayed the Lord would help you remember if it was His will."

"Remember *what* exactly? What *was* between us?" She sent a quick glance to the guard. He hadn't stopped them yet, but he was watching them with a narrowed gaze.

She forced her attention back to the ground in front of her, keeping her posture casual. As if they weren't discussing the thing that mattered most.

Ben's voice softened even more. "You caught my notice the first day you came to our school in Marcyville, and I finagled a way to see you more by helping you catch up with the rest of the class in our grade books. You didn't seem to mind spending time with me so...well, we did most everything together. You had my heart by the time summer came, but I knew we were too young. When I turned twenty, I took a job working with your uncle at the sawmill. I planned to ask you to marry me, but I wanted to request your hand from your father first."

As he spoke of his trip east to deliver his sister to a college in Pennsylvania, then a secret detour to her hometown to find her parents, a dread crept into her chest. Something awful was about to happen. Something that gripped her around the throat and wouldn't let her breathe.

"Stop." She managed to croak the word, and the guard frowned at her. But he still didn't quiet them. Could he understand what they said? Maybe he realized they weren't speaking of plans to escape.

Regardless of the reason, she refocused on Ben. "Don't say more. I can't hear it."

Quiet settled between them, allowing in the distant sounds of the village around them. Voices. Someone humming far away. Children laughing.

The normal life in a camp. As if two people hadn't been captured. As if two innocents weren't being held against their will on the other side of a thin strip of hides.

"Do you remember any of what I just said?" he asked.

She took in a deep breath and released it slowly. "I felt like I could almost grasp the memories of us studying. Maybe... sitting at a table with a book and slate?"

"Yes." Excitement slid into his tone, though he spoke quietly. "At my house. We did that almost every day."

She searched for more. Another hint of a feeling. A vague remembrance. "Maybe at a...train station?" This picture came clearer, but she couldn't find Ben in the image. "Maybe you weren't there."

"I was there." The excitement seeped out of his voice. "That was probably the day Elise and I came West."

Once more that feeling of dread crept in, though not as overwhelming as before. Should she stop him again?

But who was Elise? A woman who'd come between them? Had Ben chosen her over Heidi?

He spoke again before she could sort through the swirl of questions. "Elise is my sister. She'd heard the Indians in the western territories wanted to hear about God, so she decided she would be a missionary to them. I knew we couldn't let her go alone and...well, my presence with you there in Marcyville was putting you in danger. So I left with Elise to help her with her mission work."

His story rang true in her spirit, as though his words matched the experience she'd lived. But hurt crept in. He'd left her? Even if for her own good, had she agreed to that? She couldn't imagine choosing to allow Ben to leave forever.

"When were you to return? Or...did you send for me?"

He let out a soft breath. "I wish I'd been that courageous. I told myself you'd move on without me. That you were safe as long as I wasn't there, and you would find some other fellow who could provide for you far better than I could."

She couldn't help but look at him now. "You thought I'd be better without you?"

He lifted a gaze so deep with sorrow it made a knot ball in her chest. "I'm sorry, Heidi. With everything in me, I wish I'd chosen differently." His eyes turned glassy. "That day I met you and Temperance burying your cousin beside the Marias River was the best day of my life, though I wasn't sure of it at the time." Chagrin washed over his face. "Except for Philip. I'm truly sorry about him."

She gave a small nod. She had no memories of Philip yet, but Ben and Temperance had told her what happened. She'd surely mourned her cousin's death.

She didn't speak as her mind and heart struggled to work through all these new details. She could almost see their journey to this point. A few memories even slipped in. Whatever he'd discovered when he went to find her father felt like a murky area she didn't want to step into yet.

But now... Where did they stand *now*? Or at least, where had they stood before her fall?

She glanced at him, and he met her gaze quickly before looking forward again. She did the same as she spoke. "Did things change when you and the others joined us on this mapping assignment?" They must have. She wouldn't have been able to travel with Ben—to see him every single day—without renewing an attachment between them.

His mouth curved. "It took a while for me to regain your trust, but after I told you the truth about why I left you in Marcyville, we decided to start fresh. I asked if I could court you anew and you agreed. In fact, we had our first outing the night you fell. A walk to the river and...."

The way his voice faded meant there had likely been more than a simple stroll. Her lips burned as though they remembered the more. Maybe he'd *actually* kissed her, or maybe she'd simply wished for it. Imagined it. Either way, she had a much better idea of how things had stood between them.

But now...they had to get out of this place.

She studied the dim interior of the lodge. Night would be on them soon. Would the guard build a fire? Maybe they would be expected to simply lay down and sleep.

If there was no light in the lodge, perhaps they would have a chance to sneak out under cover of darkness. Maybe their guard would sleep. She'd have to stay awake to watch for the chance.

"Heidi?"

In the fading light, it was getting harder to see his face.

"I just want you to know that I don't expect things to be the way they were before your fall. I don't want you to feel obligated toward me in any way. I'll earn back your affections, whether it takes a month or a year. Or ten years." Pain infused his words. "Assuming we have that long. But you don't have to love me because of the past or what you think you're supposed to do. I want everything to be real between us, nothing but honesty. When you're ready, I'll be here. And every moment until then. You can take as much time as you need."

If he felt even a part of the love that coursed through her chest, those words must have taken a great deal of strength and courage to speak.

She smiled, though he might not see the expression with the lodge so dark now. "I suppose we'll have to find a way out of here so you can keep that promise."

CHAPTER 19

$\mathcal{W}$eariness weighted Heidi's eyelids as the lodge finally grew lighter with morning. She'd tried to stay awake to watch for a chance of escape, but their guard never closed his eyes. Sometime around dawn, another man came to take his place, this one older and sterner than either of the two before him.

The lodge door flap shifted now, and an Indian woman stepped inside. The buckskin dress she wore had more elaborate beadwork than anything Heidi had seen in the village where she'd met Ben. Strands of gray streaked her black braids, so her age might be close to this new guard's.

She laid a bark plate in front of Heidi first, then Ben. She spoke in her language with a nod, then turned and left the lodge.

Ben glanced from his food to Heidi's. "Pemmican, I think. Like a cake of meat and berries." It looked sort of like Aunt Bertie's fruitcake. But whether it tasted like that or not, her gnawing belly would appreciate something to fill it.

Eating once again proved challenging, especially since the pemmican was tough and hard to bite off with her hands bound to her sides. But she had plenty of time to work on it as the long morning crawled by.

Heat crept into the still lodge, especially as the sun shone through the small round opening at the top where the poles met. For a while, the stream of sunlight landed exactly on her, blinding one eye and drawing sweat as it heated her.

While the morning passed, the guard worked on sticks that looked like the start of arrows, straightening them by rubbing the wood against a small rock in his hand.

She didn't try to hide her interest as he worked. Her body craved action, but she could make no move without drawing his sharp focus. Would he allow her and Ben to talk as the younger guard last night had?

She glanced at Ben. "So...tell me about what we did back in Marcyville."

A small smile touched his eyes, but he darted a glance at the guard. She did her best not to look at him, too, or it might seem they were doing something suspicious.

Ben gave a single nod as he met her gaze. He must think it all right to talk. "We did a lot of things. I made up every reason I could to be with you. One time we were walking to my house after school and we saw a skunk. I think the poor animal was more shocked than we were. I'd never seen a skunk so close, so when it turned and raised its tail, I didn't realize what was about to happen. But you did.

"You pushed me away. Hard. Putting yourself between me and the skunk. We ran as fast as we could, but you were hit with the spray, and you stunk of it for a week, no matter how much my ma and Elise worked to get it off you and your clothes."

She could imagine the scene, and it brought a smile, despite the pressing heat and the sweat beads tickling her back. "What did my aunt and uncle say?"

He wrinkled his nose. "You were worried about telling them because you'd only lived there a few months, so I went with you to explain. Your aunt didn't seem angry, but she made you go around back to the kitchen instead of coming through the front rooms. I think she wanted to scrub you more before she let you into the family chambers."

She worked for a memory of that. Something of her aunt. She could picture what the woman looked like and was fairly certain it was recollection, not imagination. And maybe…maybe she could remember sitting in a big metal tub in a kitchen. There was a cookstove and a work counter and a dry sink…

"I've been thinking." Ben's words pulled her from the challenge of remembering, and she lifted her brows at him. "I want you to know that I firmly believe God is going to help us out of this." He flicked his eyes to her bonds. "I've been praying every minute, and He has a plan in this. He's not lost us here in this Blackfoot camp."

The burn of tears rushed into her eyes. How had Ben known that was exactly what she'd been wondering?

His own gaze glimmered as he watched her. "He's with us. Every moment. But I think He moves even closer in the hard times. All we have to do is turn to Him and He's there. Holding us. Protecting. Making a way when it feels like things are impossible. Leading us to something much better than we can imagine in the midst of the challenges."

She had to sniff to hold back her running nose, but she managed to keep the tears from falling. "I hope you're right. It's just…hard. Hard to see Him sometimes. Hard to believe He hasn't forgotten me."

Ben's eyes softened, almost like a caress. "No one could forget you. Especially not the Father Who made you so perfectly."

As his words sank in, she lost the battle with her tears. She still couldn't think of a *father* without cringing. But the way Ben spoke of God sounded nothing like the man she hated. The domineering schemer who'd made her life so miserable.

Someone new stepped into the lodge, interrupting her churning emotions. The newcomer towered above her, leering down with something close to a snarl. This was the first man who'd guarded them. The one who'd not allowed them to talk.

He turned his back to her, and when their guard rose, this new man took his place on the fur seat. He settled like a king on his throne, ruling over these two wretched subjects with his arms crossed. There would be no more talking now.

As the day stretched on, she allowed herself to doze, as much to pass the time as to relieve her exhaustion.

If Ben was right, if God hadn't lost them but had a plan for their escape, she needed to be well-rested and ready to do her part.

~

*B*elieving his own words was growing harder and harder.

Ben groaned as another night fell and their guard didn't change. This grumpy, surly brave wouldn't allow him to so much as look at Heidi, much less speak to her.

Ben had been hoping the lenient young man from last night would return. He desperately needed a chamber pot, and likely Heidi did too. Their nighttime guard would have been more likely to allow her privacy for the act. They'd only been offered a few sips of water all day, despite the heat, so that was probably why they'd been able to manage this long without attending to personal matters. This couldn't go on.

Lord, where are you? Please don't let us down. Heidi needs to see Your hand at work here. I've told her You had a plan. You do, don't You?

Of course He did. But what if it wasn't a plan for their escape? What if He intended for them to die in this place? *Please let Heidi live. Let her see You working for good in her life.*

He stayed in that prayer, letting his eyes shut as he focused on the Lord's presence. His mind tried to drift, but he called it back.

Make Yourself real to her. Draw her to You.

Once more, his thoughts attempted to shift to sounds outside, but he pulled them back to the prayer. *If there's something I should say to her, Lord, something I should do, please show me.*

A scent pricked at his awareness. Something like food cooking. Or maybe just wood smoke from a campfire. He started to turn his thoughts back to the prayer, but then realization crept in. He'd not smelled the fires from any of the surrounding lodges before, and the voices murmuring outside had grown much louder now.

Inside this lodge, darkness had settled thickly, but he could still see the guard's outline as he stood and moved to the door flap. When he pushed it aside, the scent of smoke rushed in. The light outside was much brighter, more than the tiny crescent of moon could provide.

Was there a grassfire? The way he'd been slung over his captor's horse, he'd not been able to see the lay of the land in this area.

The guard spoke to someone outside and received a rapid-fire response. The man looked back into the lodge, but the light behind him shadowed his face. Then he turned and stepped outside, letting the door flap close.

Ben's heart pounded as he surged to his feet.

"What do we do?" Heidi's voice struggled like she was trying to rise too.

His legs nearly didn't hold him, they'd grown so numb from sitting in the same position. "We have to get out of here. Can you stand?"

"I'm up, but my feet are asleep. I don't know if I can walk."

He shuffled toward the door opening, tiny arrows shooting up his legs as they came back to life. He had to see what was happening outside. Were they being left behind completely while the village escaped? Maybe the danger wasn't great, and a guard would be back for them any moment. They had to escape while they had a chance.

As he peered through the crack in the door flap, Heidi stepped beside him. Neither of them had free hands to move the curtain, so he poked his face out.

Shadows scurried everywhere, people shouting and calling things he couldn't understand. Babies cried and horses screamed in the distance.

As a backdrop to it all, the orange glow he'd glimpsed before spread across the sky in the direction of the river. The blaze of fire showed beyond the lodges.

This was early summer still, the ground moist, the grass not very brown. Not withered enough to be so flammable that it would set this blaze from a single spark. There'd been no lightning either. Meaning the fire had been lit intentionally

Something like this would have taken many people lighting many fires. And now that the inferno blazed, it would take an act of God to put it out.

He had to get Heidi out of there. "Can you walk?"

She straightened. "Let's go."

He slipped out of the lodge, then scanned every direction as Heidi stepped through the opening too. The people seemed to be running south, sideways to the blaze, not directly away from it. Maybe they were trying to get around the end of the fire line. Perhaps the lay of the land allowed better escape that direction instead of to the east, opposite the blaze.

Or maybe they thought whoever set the fire was waiting to the east, ready to swoop in and kill anyone who escaped.

If an enemy waited to the east, should he and Heidi turn north? That was the direction where White Owl and the others would be waiting, if indeed they were anticipating that Ben and Heidi could escape.

He couldn't imagine White Owl or any of the others sitting on their hands instead of doing something to free them. Perhaps *they'd* been the ones to start the fire.

He had to make a choice. North it was. "This way." He started forward, glancing back to make sure Heidi came too.

"Right behind you."

She stayed close as they wove through the camp, dodging lodges, people, and animals. No one seemed to care they were escaping. Likely, the few people still trying to flee the village were too desperate themselves.

The heat from the fire seared the side of his face, sweat running in streams down every part of him. A dog leaped in front of him, and he swerved to keep from kicking the animal.

Heidi wasn't as successful, slamming into it. She scrambled forward to catch herself, but with her arms pinned to her sides, she couldn't regain her balance. She toppled headfirst, but managed to twist so she landed on her shoulder and rolled.

Fear pressed through him. Had the blow injured her head again? She was still so fragile.

He crouched by her side, struggling to free his arms to help her, but his bonds held tight. "Are you hurt?"

She lay on her back, not moving. But he could see the reflection of the lodges around them in the glimmer of her open eyes.

"I can't..." She was squirming now. "I can't..." Desperation drove her movements as she struggled up and onto her side.

He was helpless to assist her as she gasped, still fighting to get up. "Wait, Heidi. Make sure you're not hurt before you stand." He had to get his arms free so he could carry her.

She didn't answer, just gasped again as she finally rose onto her knees, then doubled over. Finally she breathed, her body rising and falling with each inhale. She must have had the air knocked out of her. And with the rope tied so tight, there was scarcely room to draw a full breath.

As she stayed in that position, gulping in air while her

breathing slowed, he eyed the fire. The leaping flames had reached the first lodges on the western side of the village, and they rose nearly as high as the poles tied at its peak.

He and Heidi had only a few minutes left to reach the northern end of the fire line. If they didn't make it, could they turn east and outrun the blaze? *Let us make it, Lord.*

Heidi rose up, struggling to her feet. She must feel the urgency too. She surely felt the growing heat.

He stood beside her. "Can you run?"

She nodded. "Go."

He took off slowly at first to make sure Heidi kept up. Then faster. They had to reach the end of the fire line before the flames caught them.

The village gave way to grassland only broken by a few trees growing in clusters. The flame to their left engulfed a group of low cedars like a rushing river during spring thaw.

At the speed they were running, he and Heidi wouldn't make it to safety before the fire reached them. And they were slowing. No matter how hard he pushed, his legs struggled to keep pace.

They had to turn east and try to outrun the blaze. And pray there wasn't an enemy tribe lying in wait for them.

He shifted that direction. He couldn't stop to explain his reasoning to Heidi, but she'd trusted him blindly so far. Her pounding footsteps and heavy breathing barely sounded above the roar of the fire.

A scream filled the air just behind him, and a new round of panic flared through him.

He spun and nearly ran into a horse. The rider was hoisting Heidi up onto the animal, though she fought his efforts.

Ben had to save her.

Just when they were almost free, Heidi couldn't be taken from him again.

CHAPTER 20

*B*en charged forward, though with his arms bound, how could he fight?

The rider had slung Heidi over the horse's neck in front of him and now turned to face Ben. The glow of the fire illuminated the man's features, and recognition slipped through him.

The younger man who'd guarded them last night.

He'd allowed them to talk and never once growled or brandished a weapon in warning. Could it be possible he was helping them to safety?

The brave reached for Ben.

The fire had nearly arrived. If Ben didn't climb on that horse, he would die. And if he delayed the brave, Heidi would perish too.

He stepped up to the horse's side and allowed the man to hoist him up and over, halfway on top of Heidi.

As the mount started forward, his body screamed at the painful position. Heidi was probably even more miserable, but at least they were moving away from the fire. This might be the easiest position for the brave to keep them on the horse with their hands bound.

Each jolt knocked the air from him, and he could barely draw another shallow breath. The horse pushed into a canter. Where was the man taking them?

He had no idea what direction they traveled, but after a few minutes, the animal slowed to a trot so bumpy it took everything in Ben not to cry out.

They eased to a walk, and he could finally breathe. The blood had rushed to his head from hanging upside down, but when he tried to lift his chin, he could see nothing but darkness.

They'd moved far enough from the fire to be safe for a while. The horse started up an incline, and the click of its hooves proved the ground was rocky.

Lord, let him be friendly. Don't let him be taking us to kill or torture us. If the man tried to lay a hand on Heidi...the images that flashed through his mind made bile churn in his belly.

At last the horse halted, and the brave pulled up on Ben's ropes. He must want Ben to dismount.

He wiggled until he could lift his upper body and slide down the horse's shoulder. He didn't manage to get his feet beneath him, though, and tumbled backward onto to his hind end on the rocky ground.

His head swam, and he struggled to regain his senses and catch his breath.

Heidi was dismounting, too, and he managed to call out, "Careful," as her feet slid to the ground. She stayed close to the horse, leaning in as she worked to get her balance. Smart woman.

The brave studied them, and Ben worked up to his feet to face the man. Did he plan to let them go free? He still sat on his horse, not trying to restrain them.

He probably didn't speak English, but that was all Ben had to offer. "Thank you."

The man nodded as though he understood. His gaze slid to Heidi, then back to Ben. "There was one I loved. She is taken from me." He did speak English. "I did not want this to happen to you."

Goose flesh slid over Ben's arms, despite the heat. He'd understood them back in the lodge. And God used that conversation to convince the man to save them.

He smiled. "You are a good man. A brave man. I thank the great God for you and pray He gives you another to love."

Again, the warrior nodded.

As Heidi stepped back from the horse, the man pulled the knife from the sheaf at his neck and held it out. Ben moved forward and turned so the brave could cut the ropes at his arms. He had to force himself not to shift as the knife tugged at the cord, the dull edge of the metal pressing against his side.

The tie loosened, and he shook the loops free, stepping out of them. His skin burned where the ropes had rubbed, and all the strength seemed to have seeped out of his arms.

The brave did the same for Heidi, and Ben helped her pull the binding away as their rescuer replaced the knife into its holder.

Before Ben could thank him again, the man turned his horse and kicked the animal into a lope, disappearing into the darkness.

Heidi sank against his side, and he wrapped one of his tingling arms around her. He needed her support as much as she seemed to need his.

She let out a long breath. "What do we do now?"

His weary mind worked to think through where they were and what should happen next. "We need to find the others." He turned to search for landmarks that could tell him where they were. "The fire is that way." He pointed left. "It looks like we're heading into mountain country, so he might have taken us north of the fire. If that's the case, we should be able to go that way to get to the river." He pointed straight ahead.

"I guess we should start walking." Her tired tone matched his own weariness.

"Maybe we can find somewhere to sleep along the way. In the morning, we'll have a better chance of finding the others. And make sure we don't get in the middle of any more skirmishes between warring Blackfoot parties."

Heidi straightened, pulling away from him. But then her hand found his in the darkness. "Let's go."

⁓

"*M*iss Heidi? Oh, praise be. They're here!"

Heidi struggled from the clutches of sleep as the insistent voice tugged at her. When she opened her eyes, the light made her head pound. A feeling far too familiar these days. She squeezed her eyes shut again, then squinted to see what was happening.

Temperance crouched in front of her. "Heidi? Are you hurt?"

"I think she's exhausted." Ben's quiet voice sounded nearby. "At least I hope that's all it is. She's had a rough go of it."

Heidi struggled to sit up but had to grip her head to keep it from spinning. "I'm all right. What's happened?" She peered up and finally managed to open her eyes enough to see her surroundings. Ben pushed to his feet, then strode to greet White Owl and Louis and Lola.

Awareness finally settled through her.

The fire. They'd been saved. Then they'd walked until she couldn't go on. She'd sat to rest, and then...

That was the last she remembered.

She turned to Temperance with a smile. "How did you find us? What's happened? Where are we?"

Temperance returned the grin and pulled her in for a hug. The embrace was warm and tight and brought the sting of tears to Heidi's eyes. She couldn't remember Temperance being so affectionate, but she'd been such a good friend. Steady and helpful ever since the fall, and probably so much more before that. "Thank you, T," she whispered. "For everything."

Temperance pulled back and eyed her. "That's the first time you've called me T since you lost your memory. Have you got some of it back t'en?"

Another grin spilled out as the memory of her words with Ben crowded in. " Sometimes I don't even realize I've remembered something. It just comes out. Like calling you T, I suppose."

Temperance squeezed her arms. "Thank you, Jesus." Then she pulled back and turned to take in Ben and the others. "I'll bet you both are hungry. Are you hurt? Anyting need doctorin'?"

As Heidi opened her mouth, the dryness made her lips smack. "I need a drink more than anything."

"I'm sure you do." Lola stepped forward with one of the water flasks. "We prayed so hard you made it through the fire. We figured if you had, you would still be prisoners of the village that took you captive."

"How did the fire start?" Ben accepted water from Louis.

"Enemy Blackfoot not happy three braves killed. Bring back many more to set fire." White Owl still sat on his horse, Anna asleep in the saddle in front of him, cradled against his body.

Louis propped his hands at his waist. "We were watching the village for a chance to get you out. That's how we saw them start the fire. Then they spotted us and ten of them came after us. We had to retreat to the mountains, but they left us alone after that. The fire had already licked up the village though. We were praying your captors didn't leave you tied to a pole."

While Ben told of how they'd escaped and the brave who carried them to safety, Lola passed around food for them all. Heidi had never been so thankful for corncakes and smoked meat.

At last, she stood and brushed off her skirts. "I'm a smoky

mess." Soot must have been floating in the air during the fire, for her pale blue dress had darkened to navy, and smudges marred everywhere she looked, even the backs of her hands. Her face too, most likely.

"We cross mountain, then go to river to wash." White Owl motioned behind him to the north, the direction they hadn't traveled yet, if she had her bearings right.

Ben's face turned thoughtful as he studied the land where White Owl pointed. "Might be good to take a half day there to clean up and rest, then we can talk about where to go next."

Next.

They had to finish the map-making assignment. Didn't they? As she studied this group of weary, courageous friends, the idea of pushing on through even more unknown danger seemed foolish.

And for what? She could no longer summon the urgency to accomplish the assignment. If she stayed in this land with Ben, would she really need the payment for the maps?

Ben must have read her thoughts, for he stepped toward her and slid an arm around her waist. "Come on. Let's get to a place where we can clean up and rest. There will be time to sort through it all later."

~

For the first time Heidi could remember, her spirit felt at peace.

She sat next to Ben on a large boulder, worn smooth by the Marias River. She swirled her toes in the cool water, letting the liquid wash away the worries of the past days. The sun rising behind them painted the sky soft orange and pink.

They'd reached the river late yesterday afternoon, and after a swim to wash off and a warm meal, she'd slept like a dead woman. This morning, she finally felt alive again.

The memories were returning too. Not all, but the bits and pieces weren't as fragmented. No longer single images, but full scenes from events that happened the past few years.

Ben slipped his arm around her, and she leaned into him, resting her head on his shoulder. She allowed a long breath to seep out, releasing all her remaining tension with the spent air. "I wish we could stay like this forever."

He snuggled her closer. "I know."

When he spoke again, his voice rumbled beneath her ear. "I've been thinking. I'm not sure the G&F Company knew what they were sending you and Philip to do. Given all that's happened, I think it's reasonable to take them the maps you've created so far, then request a larger contingent for safety to finish mapping to the headwaters."

He squeezed her side. "I'd be happy to go explain the situation to them. You don't even have to go east. You can stay with Elise and Goes Ahead, and I'll take the maps myself. I need to get word to my family anyway. Let them know Elise and I are both well and they have grandchildren now."

The smile in his voice brought out her own, and she leaned back to look at him. "They don't know Elise is married?"

He shook his head. "We planned to send a letter with the next person we met traveling east but hadn't found anyone yet."

His expression turned sober. He was probably worried about how she would respond to his suggestion to turn back. Maybe the idea should be distasteful to her. Like giving up. Admitting defeat.

But in truth, after Philip's death and nearly losing Ben, not to mention her own fall and kidnapping...and if anything happened to White Owl or Lola or little Anna or any of them... Their group wasn't large enough to ensure their safety against the kind of threats they were likely to meet. The dangers they'd already faced.

"I don't know if I've ever spoken with anyone from the G&F.

I can't remember. I have the commission letter, but I don't know how reasonable they'll be if I return with only half the maps. Will they pay for what we've done?"

He lifted his hand and brushed the warm pad of his thumb across her cheek. "Heidi, I *want* you to be paid for what you've done. For all your hard work. But I don't want you to worry about the money."

He lowered his hand and reached for her own, weaving their fingers together. "I would be honored if you'd marry me, Heidi Wallace. I'd planned to wait until you were ready. Until you had your memories back and knew for certain you wanted me. But I've been reminded just how short life is. You can take as much time as you need to decide, but when you're ready, I don't want to wait. I want to take care of you and love you for every day we have left. You won't have to worry about earning enough from this commission to support yourself. That will be my job, forever, 'til death do us part. As soon as you'll have me."

As the words flowed from Ben's mouth, tears slipped down her face. Too much emotion built within her to stop them. Too much even to speak.

She wanted this so much. With every part of her—the parts she could remember *and* those buried so deep she hadn't yet uncovered them.

She could only nod and smile through her tears.

Maybe he understood in that way he always seemed to hear her thoughts, for he wrapped his arms around her and pulled her to his chest. Holding her tight. Securing her in his strength. In his steadiness.

Ben Lane not only *held* her heart. He *was* her heart. He was the other half God had made for her.

As she soaked in the wonderful feel of being wrapped in his love, she looked upward, to the sky that had turned a deep purplish blue.

The words Ben spoke when they were tied in the Blackfoot

lodge slipped back. *I think God moves even closer in the hard times. All we have to do is turn to Him and He's there. Holding us. Protecting. Making a way when it feels like things are impossible. Leading us to something much better than we can imagine in the midst of the challenges.*

With Ben's arms around her, she could imagine God. Not a father like who she was accustomed to. But an all-powerful being Who truly saw her. Who wrapped His arms around her and held. A God who protected and guided her toward something much better than she could see in the midst of her misery.

He'd guided her to Ben. First, all those years ago when she finally escaped life with her parents. Then in the Montana Territory, the Lord brought Ben back to her at the very moment she needed him most.

Ben was her *something much better*, and if God was a loving Father, as Ben said, she could come to love having a father like him.

Thank You...Father. She couldn't quite put the rest of her emotions into a clear thought. But if God knew everything about her, He probably knew the depth of her hope better than she did. *Thank You.*

CHAPTER 21

$\mathcal{N}$erves churned in Heidi as she sat with Temperance and Lola later that morning beneath a cluster of trees near the river. The breeze blowing across the water cooled them as much as the shade protecting them from the rays of the summer sun.

Temperance played with little Anna, counting her toes and fingers while Lola mended moccasins. Heidi had mending of her own to do, but with her body still weary and her mind so full, she wouldn't make much progress if she attempted the task.

She needed to tell these friends what she and Ben had decided—both decisions, but especially the one that pertained to the entire group.

Surely Temperance and Lola would be relieved to turn back to safety. This was definitely the right choice. The wiser path.

Yet would they think she was giving in when she should be fighting to carry on?

She took a deep breath before starting. "Ben and I talked about where we should go next."

The women looked up at her, brows raised. Such dear

friends. Both of them, though she'd not known Lola as long as Temperance.

She sent them a soft smile. "We've decided to turn back. With everything we've experienced so far on this journey, there's no telling what dangers lie ahead. You're all too important for us to risk your lives."

Anna cooed, drawing Heidi's gaze. She touched her pudgy fingers. "Especially you, little one."

When she looked up at the others, Lola reached out and took her hand. "I know that's not an easy choice. But sometimes being brave means stepping away from danger rather than running into it."

Something in those words, in Lola's quiet support, eased the angst in her chest. She squeezed her hand. "I hope this is right." She looked to Temperance. "And I hope you don't mind cutting our adventure short. We plan to go back to Elise and Goes Ahead's village, and then..." Now for the next bit of news. She took a deep breath and couldn't stop a smile as she gathered her courage. "And then, I've agreed to marry Ben. There in a little ceremony by the river."

Temperance squealed, and both women swarmed her, hugging congratulations and begging for details.

She could finally let her joy free as she shared their plans. "After that, Ben will go east to deliver the maps and tell the G&F Company they need to send a larger delegation—at least fifteen or more men for protection to finish. He'll tell them we're happy to accompany that group to draw the maps."

"So he'll be leavin' you? Right after you're wed?" Temperance sounded surprised, and for good reason. After Ben abandoned her before, Heidi had no plans to allow him to do so again. Not even for a few months.

Heidi bit her lip. "Well. I think he's planning for me to stay with Elise and Goes Ahead, but I've been thinking I'd really rather go with him."

"Of course you should. You need a wedding trip." Lola grinned.

Heidi tried to return the smile, but the weight of the other memory that had returned pressed too hard. "You're right about that. But there's another reason I want to go east, just for a short visit. I need to set a few things straight."

Lola sat quietly as Heidi told everything—the depths of her parents' sins, the scheme Ben had overheard, the price on her head. All of it.

Partway through, Temperance rubbed a hand up and down her back. A gentle reminder of her steadfastness.

Lola's expression didn't turn to disgust, though lines formed on her brow as Heidi finished.

At last, she shook her head. "I'm so sorry, Heidi. What an awful past you overcame." She reached for her hand and squeezed. "You're a remarkable woman to have come through it all with such grace."

Heidi nearly snorted. "I don't feel graceful at all." She took in a long breath and released it. "I do feel *God's* grace, though. And I'm learning to see Him as a good Father. I'm discovering what that looks like."

Temperance smiled at that, but the look turned into a thoughtful frown. "Don't you think it would be better if you did stay with Elise? Is it wise for you to risk going back to the States?"

Heidi gave a firm nod. "I may have been raised by my parents, but I've not committed the crimes they have. At least not when I was old enough to realize what they were doing. I want to set my name straight. I don't know how I'll do it, but surely the truth will prevail. I just need to find people who haven't been paid off."

"I might have an idea." Lola straightened, her eyes bright. "This could be just the thing. I have a solicitor back in Pittsburg. He was my father's attorney, but he's been handling things for me with my father's companies since I came west. He's well-connected. I can't believe the things he's able to accomplish. He knows just who to go to for whatever he needs, be it government approvals or patents or anything. He's proven trustworthy too. I'll bet he would know which of the judges were paid off and who stands firm for truth."

Once more, Heidi's heart lifted with the hope that had bloomed that morning. "Do you really think so? What of the costs though?" She certainly didn't have funds lying about to pay such a man. And Ben was the middle son of a minister with eleven children. He'd only worked in the sawmill for a year before leaving with Elise. She had no doubt he would provide for her, but he wouldn't have the kind of money they'd need for an attorney. Maybe the payment for her maps would cover it.

"My father left my brother and me a good inheritance," Lola said, "and it's just sitting in the bank in Pittsburg. I'm not using it, and neither is Caleb. I know beyond a doubt he would want it to go to a cause like this." She tipped her head. "I actually doubt there will be many costs at all. Only a simple consultation and a letter or two. Mr. Putnam will know what to do."

She nodded, the matter settled, then picked up Anna as the babe crawled into her lap.

Temperance cleared her throat, drawing Heidi's gaze. Her pale skin had turned red, as it did when she was angry or embarrassed. The tiny smile playing at the corners of her mouth didn't make her seem vexed though. She lifted her gaze, then dropped it to the grass as she picked a strand. "I suppose since we're sharing news..."

The pause made Heidi's chest tighten. Did this have something to do with Louis? He and Temperance were together often these days. Talking yes, but mostly just...together. He helped her at the cookfire. Or they stood near each other when the group stopped to rest the horses. Or they gathered firewood together.

T raised her gaze and met Heidi's, her face flaming even brighter. "Louis asked me to marry also. Once we finished helpin' you with the mappin', we aim to ride north, back to Canada and t'e fort where he once lived."

A new round of emotions swirled through her. "Oh, T."

Temperance's eyes turned glassy, and she looked almost like she was asking permission.

Heidi pulled her into a hug and sniffed back her emotions. "I'm so happy for you, but I'm going to miss you so."

Temperance clung to her, and Heidi soaked in the gift of her friendship, doing her best not to sob all over T's shirtwaist. When they pulled back, Heidi wiped her eyes.

She smiled at her friend. "He's found a treasure. You can be sure I'll make sure he knows it too."

Temperance grinned through her own dripping emotions, her self-assured sass shining through. "Oh, he knows it."

~

Heidi's chest ached as she stood beside Lola, holding little Anna as Temperance and Louis pledged their lives together. Ben stood on the other side of the couple, officiating the ceremony in a strong confident voice as he spoke the words from a small book in his hand. He looked so dashing there in his buckskins and freshly shaved face, the Marias River flowing behind him.

They'd stayed in this refuge by the water three days now, resting and catching up on chores like laundry and cooking. And preparing for Temperance and Louis to leave them.

It still didn't seem possible she would say goodbye to T tomorrow. Maybe for forever.

But the joy shimmering on her face now as she stared up at Louis eased the pain of the coming sorrow. These two were perfect for each other. Louis brought to life in Temperance a freedom that Heidi had been trying to nurture since they'd left Marcyville. Now T would fully leave her life of servitude behind.

Ben raised his hands to rest on the couple's shoulders. "Now that Louis and Temperance have given themselves to each other by solemn vows, with the joining of hands, I pronounce that they are husband and wife, in the Name of the Father, and of the Son, and of the Holy Spirit. Those whom God has joined together let no one put asunder."

He looked to Louis with a grin. "You may now kiss your bride." After giving his shoulder a playful shake, Ben stepped back.

Temperance sent a nervous grin around their group, but Louis quickly regained her attention as he took a half-step toward her.

Heidi's chest ached as he leaned down and placed the sweetest of kisses on Temperance upturned mouth. So gentle, yet the dreamy expression on T's face as he pulled back showed just how much it had affected her. Louis truly did seem to treasure this remarkable one who was now his wife.

Ben's voice slipped in to pull the couple from their locked gaze. "Please turn and face the congregation."

Louis leaned in and whispered something to Temperance, and her grin broadened as the pair turned to face White Owl, Lola, Heidi, and little Anna.

"I now present to you Mr. and Mrs. Louis Charpentier."

Heidi squealed and joined the others in clapping—as best she could with the babe squirming in her arms. As Temperance and her new husband stepped forward, Heidi moved toward her friend.

She wrapped her free arm around T's neck and pulled her in for a hug. "I am so very happy for you, my friend."

"Thank you." Temperance murmured into her shoulder, gripping her tightly. "For everything."

As Heidi pulled back, Temperance's wet eyes matched the tears clouding her own. Yet T didn't look shy or uncertain like she often did around the others. A quiet confidence marked her expression, blending perfectly with the joy that radiated from every part of her.

Heidi stepped back to allow Lola to give Temperance a hug. They would celebrate with a midday feast—White Owl had brought down a buck so fresh meat roasted over the campfire even now.

Then the newlyweds would set out to the north, to their new home in the Canadas. Tomorrow morning, the rest of them would turn south, taking a wide berth around the places where they'd met with unfriendly camps.

Could she really let Temperance set out into such an unknown life? What if they never made it to Louis's former village?

The group had started toward camp, so she turned to follow. Temperance slowed, coming alongside Heidi. Heidi slipped her arm through her friend's, propping up her smile so she didn't darken T's special day. "It was a lovely ceremony. I don't think you could have asked for a more beautiful setting."

T smiled at her, laying her hand on Heidi's as they walked. "It's not at all like I imagined my wedding day, but I like this much better."

Heidi raised her brows. "And now you're headed off on a grand adventure to places unknown. Leaving me with nary a glance behind."

The light in Temperance's eyes dimmed, making Heidi want to call back the words. Or at least give them a lighter tone. A bit of that shyness slipped into her gaze. "Louis wants to cover some ground before dark."

Heidi nudged her shoulder as she leaned in. "And a bit of privacy for the wedding night will be nice too."

T's face flared red as she dipped her chin, her teeth flashing in a grin she tried to cover.

Heidi chuckled. "I didn't mean to embarrass you." Should she say something of her worries? Maybe Temperance needed one final chance to change her mind. Everyone deserved that, surely.

She squeezed T's arm. "Seriously, though. Are you worried about venturing out into the wilderness, just the two of you?"

Temperance straightened, the embarrassment slipping from her expression. Her voice held a strong, steady power as she answered. "I'm not worried." She met Heidi's gaze, that certainty taking hold again. "I've always wanted an adventure, one I could really call my own."

Her focus slipped to Louis where he inspected one of their horses. "We're in God's hands. I trust Him and Louis both, wherever they lead me."

The ache in her chest eased, and she smiled as they fell into step again. "Well then. I guess you're ready for this adventure of yours."

As they reached the others, Temperance joined Lola in loading plates. White Owl had taken his energetic daughter to join Louis with the horses. Ben stood by the river, staring out over the water. Something about his solitude, the pensive way he studied the current, drew her toward him.

When she reached his side, he looked over with that smile that made her feel so...seen. So cherished. As though he'd been waiting all day to finally lay eyes on her.

She slipped her hand in his, and he wove their fingers together, rubbing his thumb over the back of her hand. As she turned to the river, he refocused that direction too. She leaned against his arm. "What were you thinking about?"

His voice took on a thoughtful tone. "Oh, just wondering about our future. Where it's going to take us."

She smiled. "Well, I know for sure it's taking us south tomorrow. After that? It's all unknown."

He chuckled, releasing her hand to wrap his arm around her waist and tug her closer. "It feels like the beginning of a great adventure."

As she lifted her face to his and met his smile, he pushed a strand of hair away from her face. His touch spreading a tingle through her body as he tucked the lock behind her ear.

He leaned in and brushed the gentlest of kisses across her lips, his warm breath making hers come quicker. He lingered there, pulling back just enough for her to drink him in with her gaze. "I'm ready for wherever God leads us, as long as you promise to stay by my side."

"Always." The ache of love burned through her, and with the murmur of the Marias rustling beside them, she pulled Ben closer to seal her promise with a kiss.

EPILOGUE

*B*en dipped his comb in the river and pulled it out dripping to brush through his mass of unruly brown hair. These waves never would stay straight after a trim, and Elise had cleaned up all his long angles in preparation for today. Hopefully he appeared respectable enough that Heidi wouldn't cringe when she looked at him.

Heidi.

Today was their day. This, the hour he'd been waiting for since he was fifteen years old.

The sound of footsteps rustled in the grass behind him, so he turned. Had Heidi come to talk through last minute nerves? His gut tightened. *Lord, don't let her change her mind.*

But Elise greeted him with a smile as she joined him beside the Marias. She scanned him from wet hair down to his new elaborately-beaded moccasins—a gift from Goes Ahead's mother when he and the others returned from the mapping expedition.

And this wasn't the only gift waiting when they rode into the village. Friends and friends-of-friends had come, a large group of both white and native families he and his sister had met on their journeys through the mountains.

Among them was Caleb Jackson, Lola's brother whom she came west to find, as well as his wife, Otskai, and their feisty son, River Boy. Their coming was more of a blessing than Ben could have hoped for, since Caleb had been a reverend back in Indiana and agreed to perform the marriage ceremony today for Ben and Heidi.

With Caleb's family came the other men he'd first traveled west—brothers Adam and Joel Vargas and their families, another man they simply called French and his wife and young babe. And a Peigan Blackfoot man Ben had met in one of the Nez Perce towns they'd visited—Beaver Tail, along with his wife Susannah and young son.

Ben had heard about Beaver Tail even before he met him, that he was an exceptionally wise man. When they were introduced, he could easily see why the people in that village spoke so highly of him. The man held himself with a bearing that set him apart, yet not in a proud way. It was hard to put words to what made him different. A quiet humility captured some of it. Definitely wisdom. Perhaps it was the strength of his faith that made him stand out so. That had been one of the greatest pleasures of meeting this man.

Now they were all here in this Gros Ventre village, gathering in the meadow for the marriage ceremony that would take place soon. Hopefully Elise could help him hurry things along.

He waited, brows raised, as Elise finished her inspection of him.

At last she nodded. "I think you'll do." She stepped forward and brushed something off his sleeve.

He swallowed, trying to read Elise's expression. She'd been helping Heidi prepare, had probably just come from his bride-to-be. "Is she...nervous?"

Elise's features softened as she met his gaze. "She's excited. She keeps asking if you're ready to start the ceremony yet."

He straightened. "Yes. Let's do it." He bent and scooped up his kit.

Elise chuckled, and as he straightened, she pressed a hand to his arm. "Wait, Benji."

He paused, meeting her gaze. Her eyes had turned glassy. Was something wrong? Had Heidi asked her to tell him something she couldn't bring herself to say to him directly? His chest gripped tighter. "What is it?"

She sniffed. "I'm sorry, I just…" She gave an effort toward a smile. "It seems wrong somehow, you being married so far away from our family. They're not here to celebrate with us."

His muscles eased, and he let out a breath. Not a problem with Heidi then. Just Elise's nerves.

He dipped his chin so he was on a level with her. "It seems I'm not the first to be married so far from home, too far away for the family to even know of the wedding."

His teasing worked, for a real smile broke through her worried expression. Reminding her of Goes Ahead and the children always brightened her mood. She bit her lip, but the effort didn't hold back her grin. "I guess you're right."

He reached for her, tugging her into his arms. "It's all right big sister. You've been a good mama for me out here. I'm growing up though. You're going to have to loosen the apron strings a little."

"Oh, you." She gave his arm a playful swat. But then she wrapped her arms around his waist and clung. "It's just hard to let go sometimes."

He held her a second, then pushed her back. She needed a bit more teasing so she didn't work herself back into a stir. "I bet you'll be glad to hand over the raising of me to another woman. Remember how much trouble I gave you when I was a baby? How I cried and cried any time you put me down?"

She rolled her eyes. "You were a trial, no doubt about it."

He wrapped an arm around her shoulders and started them walking toward the meadow where the ceremony would be held. "Remember how hard it was to teach me my letters? Ma tasked you with making sure I was ready to start school, and I think I brought you to tears more than once."

"If you'd simply focused on my instruction, you'd have learned in a day. You wouldn't stop wiggling and spinning circles and making silly faces."

He snorted. "It's a wonder I ever learned to read."

"No doubt." She huffed. "Now that I think on it, I *am* glad to hand over your care to Heidi. Maybe she can manage you better than I have."

He squeezed her shoulders. "You'll have to give her some tips along the way, I'm sure."

His big sis sent him a grin. "No doubt."

~

*I*f Heidi hadn't spent so much time around White Owl, she might have been nervous when Susannah and Beaver Tail stepped into the lodge where she waited for Elise to come get her for the ceremony.

She'd met them both when she, Ben, Lola, and White Owl returned from the mapping expedition. She'd another white woman to be in these parts, but Susannah and Beaver Tail seemed perfectly suited to each other. And their son was precious—a boy not quite two years old. From the swell across Susanna's middle, it looked like they'd have another little one joining them in a few months.

Now, Beaver Tail and Susannah stood before her, a smile sparkling on the woman's face that brimmed with expectation. "I hope you don't mind, but we brought you something. A gift that's considered very special among his family when given to a bride."

Heidi lifted her gaze to the man as he stepped forward. His bearing had struck her before as both noble and understated, but now his eyes held a kindness she wouldn't have expected.

"The white fox is not often seen in the warm days. When one crossed our path on the journey to this place, I knew it was a gift from Creator Father for something to come. When we learned of the joining that is to happen this day, I knew in my spirit this was to be yours. A reminder that Creator Father goes with you always. He is the center of this joining, to strengthen the tie between you."

Her chest squeezed and tears stung her eyes, but she smiled through them as she accepted the fur. These people barely knew her, yet they cared enough to give her such a gift. And the blessing his words had bestowed upon her marriage with Ben..."Thank you."

Her fingers sank into its softness, a feeling she'd not expected. She brushed her hand down its snowy length. "This is remarkable." She raised her gaze to Beaver Tail, then took in Susannah. "Thank you so much. You can't know what this means to me."

She'd met so many people in this land who'd surprised her. Who'd changed her life. Ben of course, but White Owl and Lola too. And Elise and Goes Ahead. Even Goes Ahead's parents, who'd been such kind hosts. She'd never felt quite as at home as in this Gros Ventre village tucked away hundreds of miles from anything she'd ever known.

Hopefully, she and Ben could come back to this place after they went east to clear her name.

A knot of nerves tightened her belly at the thought of what might come in that endeavor. But she pushed the worries away.

Elise was entering the lodge, and they all turned to her. She met Heidi's gaze with a twinkle in her eye. "Ben and

Caleb are ready. The congregation's gathered too. It's your turn."

A flurry of excitement swept through her middle as she followed Elise out of the lodge. They wove their way through the maze of homes to the open meadow beside the river where they'd chosen to hold the ceremony.

So many people had gathered, faces turned to her with expectant smiles. She couldn't remember every name, but the kindness in their eyes made her throat squeeze.

But then her gaze found Ben and Caleb, standing beyond the others with the river behind them. Ben looked so handsome, there with the expanse of blue sky behind him. She quickened her step. Every part of her longed to reach him. To feel the warmth of his gaze sweep over her, the way his love wrapped around her, drawing her closer.

God had brought Ben into her life when she needed him most—both times. And now, Lord willing, they wouldn't be parted again. Not ever.

When she reached him, he grasped both her hands, tugging her closer, almost to his chest. She couldn't help but respond to his grin, smiling back like the lovesick woman she was.

He leaned down and his breath brushed her ear as he spoke. "Feels like I've been waiting forever, but you were worth the wait."

Heat swept up her neck, but his grin flashed more. She squeezed his hands to let him know she felt exactly the same.

Then together, they turned to face the minister. Just getting to this point had been far more adventure than she'd planned for. But whatever lay ahead, they'd have their Heavenly Father in the center of this union, strengthening the tie between them.

Though this day had been long in coming, their experiences had changed them into the people God knew they needed to be —the best versions of themselves united together. And Ben had been worth the wait.

∽

I pray you loved Ben and Heidi's story!
Would you like to receive a **free bonus epilogue about their trip back east to clear Heidi's name?**
Get the bonus epilogue and sign-up for insider email updates at
https://mistymbeller.com/JOTMP-bonus-epilogue

∽

*I*f you enjoyed this book, I think you'll also love my new series!

In the wilds of the Montana Territory, the Jericho Collins and his five brothers guard a precious secret: the hidden Sapphire mine on their ranch. Bound by loyalty, they allow no outsiders—until two mysterious sisters appear. One claims to be a mail-order bride, while the other, Dinah Wyatt, is a skilled doctor needed when tragedy strikes one of the brothers.

As suspicion and intrigue engulf the ranch, sparks fly between the enigmatic Jericho Collins and the lady doctor. In a world where trust is scarce and secrets wield immense power, can these two stubborn hearts defy the odds?

Turn the page for a sneak peek of book 1 in the Brothers of Sapphire Mountain Ranch series.

CHAPTER ONE

The wildness of this mountain territory should make Dinah Wyatt turn and usher her sister right back to Fort Benton and the first steamship to the States. But something in this grandeur —the wide open blue sky, the pine-covered slopes rising on either side, the narrow creek murmuring beside the path where she and her sister rode—brought to life a part of her she hadn't known lay dormant. This late-summer day wasn't hot and muggy like Virginia. The sun felt glorious and a light breeze cooled any excess heat.

This would be the perfect place for Naomi to settle, *if* her new husband was a good man like he sounded in his advertisement.

Of course, a man could easily lie on paper, even easier than with his lips.

But his heartfelt words had encouraged them to seek God's direction about whether Naomi was the right bride for him. The two of them had done that. Dinah herself had spent many hours beseeching the Lord—first begging for answers about why Naomi had let herself yield to temptation in the first place, then why God had felt it necessary for that sin to produce a child. When she prayed about whether this trip to the Montana Territory had been the right direction for them both, she'd finally felt a peace. A settling in her spirit that she could cling to when the doubts crept in.

As they did now.

She forced herself to ease out a long breath. They were so very far from home and all they'd ever known. Not that her sister could stay in Wayneston anymore, and Dinah couldn't allow her to take this journey alone. They'd been born together —only three minutes apart—and the one night Dinah had abandoned her sister, the worst had happened to her. She wouldn't make that mistake again.

Now both she and Naomi would learn the true character of the man they'd both traveled nearly three months for Naomi to marry—if they ever found this Collins Ranch he'd described.

Dinah straightened in her saddle and steeled her resolve. She would make sure Jericho Collins would be a suitable match for her sister and a good father for the coming babe before she found her own place in this land. Hopefully there was a quiet town nearby that wasn't consumed with gold fever where she could hang out a shingle for her clinic.

A grunt from behind made her turn. Naomi smiled from her own saddle, but the look made Dinah's chest tighten. She was only five months into her term, but she'd swelled so much during the last part of their journey. So many hours in the saddle since they left the steamboat in Fort Benton three weeks ago had taken its toll. How much more could Naomi endure?

Dinah made sure they only rode half days, allowing Naomi plenty of time to rest with her legs propped up. But still the bloating had increased. The puffiness in her face made it appear she'd doubled her weight. And panic had twisted in Dinah's chest when Naomi hadn't been able to squeeze her feet into boots. At least she'd felt the babe move again that morning. But surely the mother's suffering would have an effect on the unborn child. Her sister desperately needed time to rest in bed. Days, or maybe weeks, on her back with her feet raised on pillows.

If they didn't find that respite for Naomi at the ranch, what could they do? Maybe they should set up camp beside this stream and settle in until Naomi's swelling lessened.

Lord, let us reach this ranch today. Let Jericho Collins be the man my sister needs. A man who will care for her as the treasure she is. And her baby too.

She guided her gelding as the path crossed the creek, the animal's hooves splashing in the shallow water. Behind her, Naomi's horse crashed with a heavier stride, dislodging pebbles with each step.

"Who's that?"

The tension in her sister's voice made Dinah jerk her gaze up to the trail in front of them.

About twenty strides away, a figure stepped from the trees. He wore a leather costume similar to many they'd seen since Fort Benton. From this distance, she couldn't make out features, only broad shoulders and a bearded face.

Did he have weapons? At least he wasn't brandishing a gun that she could see.

Could this be Naomi's intended? Her pulse picked up speed. She couldn't tell his age yet, but he didn't look as respectable as she'd hoped for her sister.

He stood still, watching them approach. When they'd closed half the distance between them, he raised his chin. "You need something?"

She fought the urge to glance at her sister. Instead, she made her voice sound friendly. "We're looking for the Collins Ranch." Should they say who they were? Better to find Mr. Collins first.

He studied them, his scrutinizing gaze doing its best to make her nervous, though she fought the feeling. "What do you want there?"

Before she could answer, Naomi reined her horse up beside Dinah's. "I'm here to be Mr. Jericho Collins's wife."

Dinah tensed, cringing inside. Just because Naomi had made peace with her situation as a mail order bride didn't mean Mr. Collins wanted his private affairs broadcast to all his neighbors.

A flash of surprise flickered in the man's dark gaze. Then he sobered, eyeing them warily. "Jericho's not looking for a wife, and this isn't the Collins ranch."

Dinah frowned. He sounded as though they'd insulted him. He could at least point them in the right direction.

She opened her mouth to ask, but Naomi cut in once more. "Can you tell us where to find him? He sent for us—for me— and we've come all this way to accept his proposal."

Dinah slid a look to tell her to hold her tongue, but as Naomi met her gaze, a shout echoed in the distance.

She spun to find the source. Somewhere in the trees the man had stepped from.

Again, the voice came, far enough away she had to struggle to distinguish words. "Help...hurt."

She couldn't make out the name spoken.

The man in front of them spun and charged back into the trees.

Dinah's chest thundered and she plunged her heels into her gelding's sides. If there were injuries, they would need her.

As she rode through the woods, she had to duck under branches and swerve around trunks. Her horse caught up with the man quickly, and she reined down to a trot to follow.

At last, the trees opened into a clearing where two horses stood hitched to a wagon stood. A man knelt beside the rig, and the stranger she'd been following sprinted to his side.

A body lay before them. Not moving, from what she could tell.

She reined her horse hard and jumped to the ground. Naomi rode up behind her, and Dinah called out as she ran to the patient. "Naomi, get my case."

The men knelt on one side, so she positioned herself on his other.

The man they'd met at the stream held out one arm. "Lady, you'd better—"

"I'm a doctor." She had no time for the fellow's opinions, so she started her assessment. The patient's chest rose and fell in a steady rhythm. Harder than a resting rate, which could be from pain or shock.

Dinah looked at the man who'd been here at first. "What happened to him?"

"The wagon backed over him. I think over his leg. Not sure why he won't wake up." His voice sounded frantic.

She scanned the length of the injured man for blood. None visible, his face had paled, and a sheen of sweat glimmered from his skin.

She turned her attention to his lower half. His leather trousers bulged in the middle of his left thigh. She ran her fingers over the spot, and the man flinched, even in his unconscious state. A fracture in the body of the femur most likely. Not good, but at least no damage to other limbs that she could see.

A sneaking suspicion began to creep in. She slid a look to his face again, then pressed fingers to his cheek.

Cold and clammy. She shifted those fingers to the corroded artery in his neck. Pulse light, but racing. That matched her own heart rate, but she wasn't in nearly the same condition as this man.

Naomi puffed as she dropped down at her side with the medical case and began unfastening the buckles to open the pouch.

She needed to make sure her sister didn't overtax herself through this emergency, but the man before them was in far more danger at present. His body had begun to tremble. "He needs blankets."

"I'll get mine." Naomi pushed up to her feet.

She glanced at the two men kneeling across from her. "I need to see this leg. Does either of you have a knife?" She could cut his pants open at the thigh with her surgical blade, but she'd rather not dirty it if there was another tool available.

Both men studied her, gazes wary. A look so similar they had to be brothers. The first man who'd found them at the creek must be the elder of the two, unless the thick growth of beard covering much of his face simply made him look so. The other fellow wore his beard much shorter, as if he'd recently shaved.

Neither man offered up a knife.

Frustration clenched inside her. "I'm not going to cut his leg open, I just need to see inside the pant leg to tell if the bone pierced the skin."

The older brother's gaze narrowed even more.

She glared. "I'm a doctor. I've served six years at the side of Richmond's finest physician. I know what I'm doing here. If I don't work quickly, this man could bleed to death. Maybe we'll be lucky enough that the bone broke through the skin and the blood is flowing out. Otherwise he's bleeding internally, and I'll need to make an incision to release the flow before his organs drown in bone marrow."

The younger looked to his brother, questioning, but Scruffy Beard never took his eyes off her face. Thankfully though, he finally withdrew a hunting knife from his waistband and held it out to her.

She grabbed the handle and moved in to slice the leather encasing the injured thigh. The blade was sharp, so it cut through the leather without catching.

"Here are blankets." Naomi dropped the load of covers beside her.

Dinah didn't shift her focus from parting the buckskin. "Cover his upper body to get him warm."

When she had a full view of the bulging thigh, her insides clenched. The skin wasn't pierced, and it had turned dark purple and swollen to twice the size of her fist. She had to let out the blood pooling in there. She'd need to set the bone, too, so an incision would have to be made and soon.

She raised her head to study the landscape around them. "Is there a house here? Somewhere close we can take him?" Hopefully a place that would be more sanitary than lying here in the dirt.

The men looked at each other again, then the older brother spoke. "We can take him in the wagon to the house. It's about a quarter hour up the mountain."

She eyed the conveyance beside them. Bumping in that would move the bone even more, perhaps pinching the femoral artery, which would practically ensure the man bled out if she didn't stop the problem immediately.

She searched the area for another option, and her gaze caught on a wooden structure tucked into the edge of the woods. "What about that? Is it clean inside?"

"No." For once, the bushy-beard man answered quickly. "It's dirty and full. There's no floor."

That wouldn't do then. She turned back to her patient and his swollen purple leg. "I need a blanket to put under this."

The brothers helped her lift the leg while she held the broken section, then slipped the cloth under. While they worked, she gave Naomi instructions for what to pull out of her case. Thankfully, her bag held enough basic supplies that she would be able to bandage the incision and splint the legs together. That should hold until they got man back to the house.

At last, she pulled out her surgical blade and pulled the cut leather farther back from the swollen area.

"Wait." The older brother spoke, and she paused, looking up at him.

His dark eyes studied her, worry darkening them even more. "What are you going to do?"

Of course he would want the details. Back in Wayneston, she would have taken time to inform the patient's family of her plans. She lowered the blade. "See this dark area? His femur— um, thigh bone—is broken. It's a break significant enough to release blood and marrow from inside the bone, and it's pooling here. I'm going to make an incision, release the blood so it doesn't spread into his organs and drown them, and then set the bone pieces back into place. After that, I'll suture the incision and tie his legs together as a brace until we get him to his bed." She'd need to reset the leg with traction at that point, but she could explain when the time came.

She turned to Naomi. "Can you prepare a needle and thread?"

Naomi nodded and set to work, so Dinah returned her focus to her patient. Though his eyes remained closed, he flinched and shifted around a bit. Probably the pain and blood loss kept him from being fully aware of what was happening. That would work in his benefit for this next part.

She leveled a serious look at both men. She'd need their help. "Hold his shoulders and feet so he doesn't move. One of you at each end, please."

Thankfully the men positioned themselves as requested. Before she began, she lifted her eyes to the heavens.

Guide my hands, Lord. Let me do good, not harm.

Get book 1 of the Brothers of Sapphire Mountain Ranch series at your favorite retailer!

Did you enjoy Ben and Heidi's story? I hope so!
**Would you take a quick minute to leave a review where you
purchased the book?**
It doesn't have to be long. Just a sentence or two telling what
you liked about the story!

To receive a free book and get updates when new Misty M.
Beller books release, go to https://mistymbeller.com/freebook

ALSO BY MISTY M. BELLER

Honor in the Mountain Refuge

Peace in the Mountain Haven

Grace on the Mountain Trail

Calm in the Mountain Storm

Joy on the Mountain Peak

Brides of Laurent

A Warrior's Heart

A Healer's Promise

A Daughter's Courage

Hearts of Montana

Hope's Highest Mountain

Love's Mountain Quest

Faith's Mountain Home

Texas Rancher Trilogy

The Rancher Takes a Cook

The Ranger Takes a Bride

The Rancher Takes a Cowgirl

Wyoming Mountain Tales

A Pony Express Romance

A Rocky Mountain Romance

A Sweetwater River Romance

A Mountain Christmas Romance

ABOUT THE AUTHOR

 **Misty M. Beller** is a *USA Today* best-selling author of romantic mountain stories, set on the 1800s frontier and woven with the truth of God's love.

Raised on a farm and surrounded by family, Misty developed her love for horses, history, and adventure. These days, her husband and children provide fresh adventure every day, keeping her both grounded and crazy.

Misty's passion is to create inspiring Christian fiction infused with the grandeur of the mountains, writing historical romance that displays God's abundant love through the twists and turns in the lives of her characters.

Sharing her stories with readers is a dream come true for Misty. She writes from her country home in South Carolina and escapes to the mountains any chance she gets.

Connect with Misty at <u>www.MistyMBeller.com</u>

CPSIA information can be obtained
at www.ICGtesting.com
Printed in the USA
BVHW081024040423
661729BV00002BA/229